HAPPY DAYS

N. D. MELLEN

Published in the United States of America

ISBN 978-1-962569-58-3 (SC)

N.D. Mellen
222 West 6th Street
Suite 400, San Pedro, CA, 90731
www.stellarliterary.com

Order Information and Rights Permission:

Quantity sales. Special discounts might be available on quantity purchases by corporations, associations, and others. For details, contact the publisher at the address above.

For Book Rights Adaptation and other Rights Permission.
Call us at toll-free 1-888-945-8513 or send us an email at admin@stellarliterary.com.

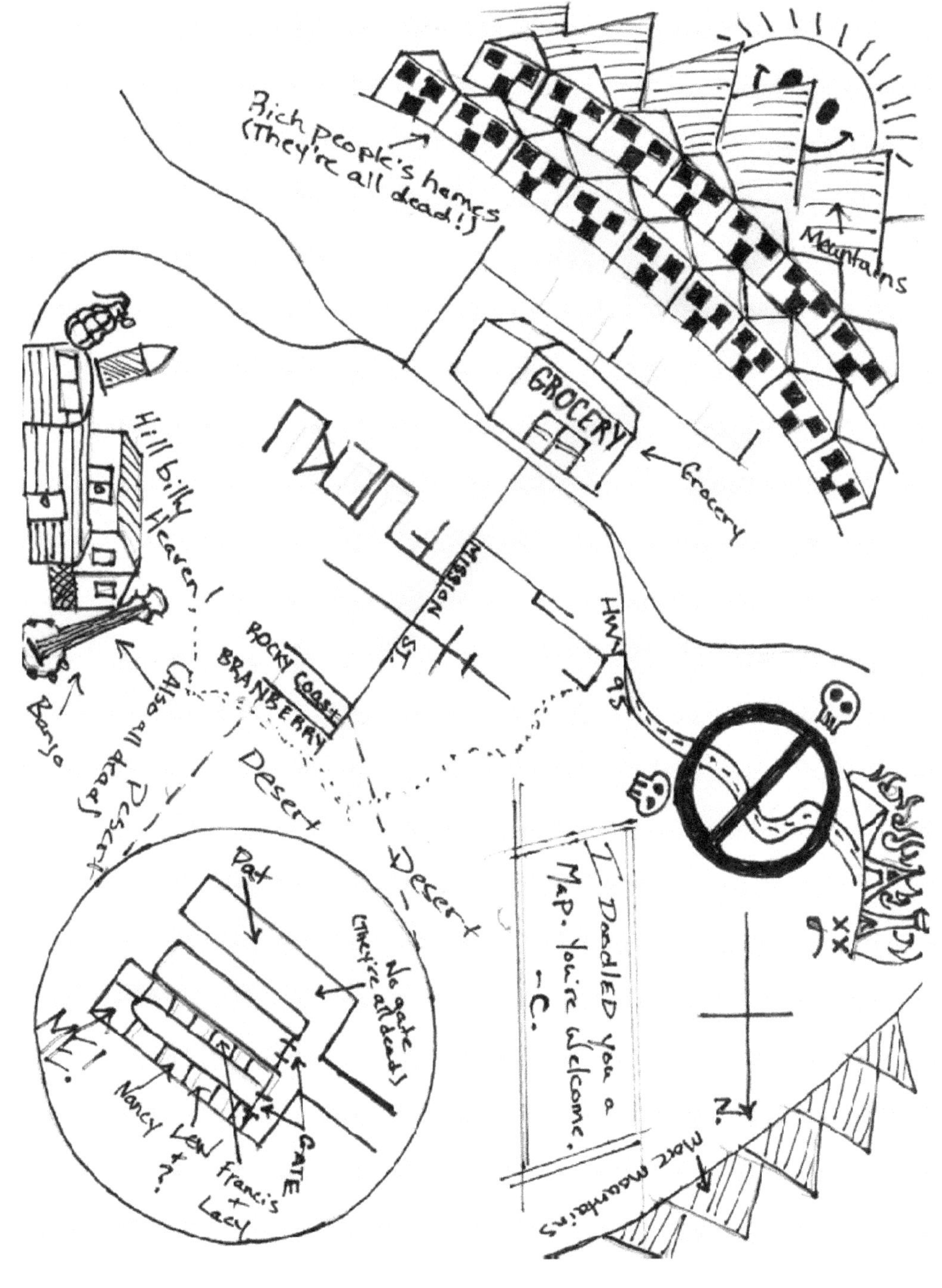

Rich People's homes
(They're all dead!)
Mountains
GROCERY
Grocery
Hillbilly Heaven!
Banjo
(Also all dead)
Desert
ROCKY Coast
BRANBERRY
Desert
MISSION ST.
HWY 95
FUCK!
Pat
No gate (they're all dead)
ME!
Nancy Len + ?
Francis + Lacy
GATE
I Doodled you a Map. You're Welcome. —C.
N
XX
More mountains

Before we begin, I need you to do one thing: check your underwear. I'm not kidding. Slide your hand down your ass cheek, and finger the material that provides a boundary between your pants from your butt. Feel the material; roll it between your thumb and forefinger. I don't care whether you wear boxers or briefs; granny panties or some lacy thong. You're the only one that knows the answer to this question:

Do you have your big boy panties on?

I won't waste time going over the details, but hear me and understand: this isn't a happy story. Romeo and Juliet don't reunite in the end, mighty Paladins of Virtue don't overcome all, and people die. Actually, almost everyone is dead already, but who's counting?

So. You've had a moment to regard your constitution and check the level of your political correctness. If you feel like you can handle a story with no frills beyond the actual events, then read on. Just don't expect a hero. After all, good guy, bad guy … it's all just a matter of perception.

It didn't start with an atomic war; it didn't start with bodies crawling out from the earth. It wasn't Captain Tripps, from some Stephen King novel. It certainly wasn't some government fuck up that caused the release of some black cell virus. Honestly, I wouldn't give the government that much credit.

When the zombie apocalypse started, it began with ants.

Sounds stupid, right? Wait, though; hear me out, and I promise it will all make sense. Our records are understandably a bit shady, but here's how it happened as best as we can tell:

In the waning months of 2014, "Ant Killer Pro!" was released to the market of consumers on late night television for the *"Low, Low Price!"* of 29.99. It guaranteed to not only kill ants, but to leave a residue that would keep them away from your home forever. FOREVER! MONEY BACK GUARANTEE!

BUT WAIT! THERE'S MORE!

Not only would it keep ants away from your home forever, but the other pests that preyed on them or ate their bodies- spiders, flies and the like- would also consume the toxin and NEVER- *EVER-* COME BACK!

Now, I want you to keep that in mind for a moment. I'm going to tell you another story, and then we'll get back to the ants.

I want you to imagine a little girl. Make her look any way that you want her to: blond hair, black hair; white, Chinese, black. It doesn't matter; just make sure that she's a little girl. Now, imagine that Little Girl's parents aren't too well off. They're a young couple, and while they do their best to be frugal and buy cheap, they still find it hard to make ends meet. Like most young parents starting out, though, they can't resist a bargain. After all, most parents know that Pampers are better than Huggies, but if you can get 33% more Huggies diapers at two- thirds the price? That's a no brainer.

With that mindset, it's easy to understand why Little Girl's parents chose to eat where they ate one average afternoon: a somewhat seedy, hole in the wall Japanese joint that was advertising Asian chicken wings at five cents apiece. Little Girl's parents were stoked at their good fortune. Lunch dates were luxuries that they couldn't really afford, but at five cents a wing? *That* they could do; that was a bargain.

The family of three had a grand time. They ordered thirty wings, and managed to eat twenty one of them between them. Mommy and Daddy even went so far as to splurge on a happy hour beer at $2.50, which they shared. The remaining nine wings were wrapped up in tin foil made to look like a swan, meant to be enjoyed as a late night snack later that evening. It was a wonderful day filled with laughter and the almost forgotten sense that the problems of today weren't so bad; tomorrow would be better, for sure. Little Girl had been on her best behavior, and that had allowed Mommy and Daddy a brief reprieve to feel young and carefree again.

What Mommy and Daddy didn't know was that the chicken wings weren't chicken wings; they were pigeon wings. And not just any type of pigeon; they were dirty, city pigeons. The type of pigeons that had already managed to survive any number of poisons and traps laid out by local exterminators; pigeons that had survived every assault, shrugging off the effects of the inept trappers and bulking up their avian immune systems every day. The one trap that they couldn't avoid?

The owners of a seedy Japanese restaurant in a seedy neighborhood that advertised chicken wings at five cents apiece.

The bait that the owners used? Tempura puffs laced with arsenic, strychnine, and a variety of other flavorful poisons that hailed from the land of the Rising Sun. The pigeons ate'em up in droves, and died with little bird smiles on their beaks while they shit their innards out. A daily gathering, a quick plucking of feathers by an experienced hand, and into the fryer they went.

Now here-*here*- Late Night Buyer, is where our stories converge.

Having eaten their fill of fried pigeon, Little Girl and her parents returned to the small apartment that they rented. The neighborhood was a bit run down, but Little Girl's parents had done their research. They were poor, not stupid, and had found a friendly- if somewhat dilapidated- complex within walking distance of the local military base. Filled with mostly military guys in their early twenties, the complex could get a bit noisy at times, but all of the residents were friendly enough. And besides, Little Girl's parents must have thought, we're surrounded by soldiers; can't get much safer than this, right?

Little Girl's stomach was full as she labored up the stairs to their little apartment, bloated to the point of pain. She didn't say anything, though, because she didn't want to ruin The Good Day. She was holding Mommy's finger, using it to assist her up the stairs. Mommy was patient about it because she couldn't pick Little Girl up; her right arm was full of the carryout bag from lunch.

Little Girl misplaced a step, canting to the side and almost stumbling as she heard a cheerful cry from Daddy. Daddy had walked ahead of them, walking easily up the stairs with her monkey face backpack slung over his shoulder. Shocked as she was by the abrupt crow, Little Girl liked the sound. Daddy was great at everything- He loved her and played with her, and she loved and played right back- but he didn't laugh very often. He spent more time worrying about his friend Bill, and how he was going to pay him.

As she crested the final stair, Little Girl saw the object of Daddy's sudden happiness: a small brown box covered in labels with complicated bars, sitting on the door mat to their apartment. Daddy opened it up, ruffled through the sponges of white popcorn, and came out with a metallic bottle covered in letters. Little Girl didn't know this, but the label proudly proclaimed "Ant Killer Pro!"

$29.99 was a lot to spend for Mommy and Daddy, but this stuff was *the best!* What Mommy and Daddy didn't know was that- if things had stayed the same- the product would have been recalled in the first few months, with nothing more to show for it but a handful of lawsuits involving cancer and radiation poisoning. They'd made the splurge, though, deeming it necessary. Old and run down as it was, their apartment had an ant problem. Little Girl was covered in ant bites from the waist down; red, angry things that she scratched bloody no matter how much Mommy trimmed her nails.

But Daddy was happy, and that made Little Girl happy. He wasted no time twisting the nozzle, and began spraying the toxic poison around the floor boards and corners where the ants had a tendency to congregate in their meandering lines. It had been a Good Day, and despite her aching stomach- the lining of which had begun to erode- Little Girl went to bed easily that night while Mommy and Daddy gnawed at the cold take out that they had brought home with them.

Little Girl's belly felt much better the next day; she couldn't feel it at all, in fact. But she was bored, and boredom was far, far worse than pain. Mommy and Daddy were both home from work, and she was exploring the small balcony that served as her backyard. Little Girl didn't mind the small enclosure; to the contrary, she liked the porch. It was her play place. It was a bit crowded on that day, though.

Like most young couples in their first apartment, Mommy and Daddy had a tendency to put tied bags of trash on the balcony. The black community dumpsters were simply too far away to walk down all those stairs. Little Girl didn't mind that her space had been invaded; it was quite the opposite. The tied generic Glad bag had produced a new curiosity. A corner of the cheap plastic had torn open, letting some of the trash fall out, most relevant of which was a handful of pigeon wing bones that had been consumed under the guise of chicken wings. Even better than that, though? There was a thick line of ants working their way back and forth across the floor to the half gnawed bones.

Unlike most children, Little Girl loved ants. I couldn't have told you why, and she probably couldn't have, either. But the myriad bite marks on her legs that so concerned Mommy and Daddy? They weren't from being bitten while sleeping in the comfort of her own bed; they were because Little Girl would stuff handfuls of ants into her pockets when Mommy and Daddy weren't looking. Once again, I couldn't tell you why. Maybe she wanted to bring them home; maybe she wanted pets that Mommy and Daddy couldn't provide.

But *that* day on the porch, the ants were something else; something a little different than she was accustomed to seeing. They were bloated, bigger than normal, and their tiny march was much faster than usual as they swarmed back and forth over the desiccated pigeon bones. Little Girl was immediately entranced, and reached a pudgy hand out to pluck a few up and place them in the safe confines of her pocket for later examination.

From what we understand from rumor, though, is that these weren't normal ants anymore. What the infomercials for "Ant Killer Pro!" never mentioned to the consumer was that- in the first day after consumption- these tiny, itty bitty bugs became aggressive enough to put Africanized bees to shame.

To the best of my knowledge we don't have much in the way of scientists anymore, but the general consensus from news mongers in those last few days of civilization was that the chemicals killing the ants somehow combined with the poisons on the scraps of flesh clinging to the pigeon bones. Those toxins merged. There was a reaction, and then there was an infection.

As Little Girl reached her hand down the trail of ants didn't respond as it should have. The line didn't scatter in a thousand different directions, leaving her to grasp her reaching fingers at the few that she could grasp. No; the ants *attacked* her.

They swarmed over Little Girl, climbing up her stocking legs faster than she could shriek. I'd imagine that she jumped up and down, trying to shake them off, but- one way or the other- she eventually ran from the patio and into the concerned arms of Mommy and Daddy. Her parents did their best to brush the ants off, I'm sure, but did nothing but provide a living bridge to the mindless, poisoned creatures swarming over their daughter. The tiny insects ran across their joined arms, biting, stinging; injecting the random and unforeseen composition of poison and venom into their bare skin.

Mommy and Daddy would follow the same course as Little Girl, but Little Girl is the one that could- by scientific terms- be called "Patient Zero;" the rough equivalent to Typhoid Mary.

Little Girl's name was Maggie, and she was almost four years old.

Before things went ass up, zombies were all the rage. By the later part of 2015, I didn't know of anyone that hadn't watched at least one TV episode, witnessed one movie, read one book on their iPads, Kindles, or Netflix.

I guess you couldn't really call it a sudden phenomenon. The walking dead had been a niche center of interest since, shit, I dunno, the 1960's? *Night of the Living Dead?* The entire concept was terrifying and intriguing, but ultimately asinine. Seriously, who could be afraid of lumbering corpses moving at a rate of three feet per minute? I mean, c'mon, just walk away from them.

It wasn't until shows like *The Walking Dead,* movies like *Zombieland,* or books like *World War Z* came out that your average late night consumer got an actual idea of how dangerous they could actually be. Entire cities wiped out in the span of a few hours. Small, ragged bands of survivors hiding in treehouses. The complete breakdown of society.

I gotta call bull shit on a lot of it.

I will say this, though: when the combination of poisons that created an infection- that the immune system couldn't stop, that *then* worked its way onto a military base full of Marines- really took off, it took off fast. The gestation period wasn't immediate, but when the poison found a home, people started to turn as fast as a field of fleshy egg shells opening like a scene from an "Aliens" movie. Back when we had movies, that is.

I don't know if you could really call them "zombies," per se- at least by the definition of what the movies and TV shows and books had told us- but that's what they were eventually called anyway. Personally, I blame the media for that little tidbit of propaganda.

Reports started out small, a simple outbreak of "something" at a military base in San Diego. Camp Pendleton, I think it was. Local news stations picked it up, giving vague accounts of it being a strand of tuberculosis that the CDC had never seen before. A few days after that it was rabies, maybe even an odd strain of mad cow disease. High end networks took over, highlighting the evening news, and began to label it as "infectious cannibalism."

You get where I'm going with this, right?

It wasn't long before the term "zombie" was used, and society ate it up like pizza on a Friday night ... or a Tuesday night ... hell; Monday lunch. All the Cretins swallowed it whole, sitting glued to their screens as the poison spread at an expeditious pace. Some neighborhoods decided to protest the infection of their neighbors, choosing to loot and vandalize the homes of the sick and turning as a form of resistance.

Notable public speakers in five thousand dollar suits got on screen and implored every watcher to "stop the violence." Hell, the President himself stood behind his regal dais and intoned that "change was coming."

I still wonder if our dead president knew how right he was when he said that.

Now, like I said, the gestation period was gradual and hard to predict- it could be anywhere from two days to two weeks- but once it got going it was like a spark on dried tinder. It ripped its way across the country, eating- literally, eating- and infecting most of the people that it came into contact with. This is an area where TV, and the books, and the movies got it wrong. See, according to TV, every single person on the face of the continent should have broken out in mass panic. In our neighborhood it didn't really happen like that.

Most people continued to go about their daily lives: working and drinking, smoking pot, playing video games, teaching their kids, and listening to any of the vomit that the internet spewed up … back when we had internet, that is. It only ever became a real issue when "The First Case" popped up in your state, your city, and then your neighborhood.

People didn't panic, at first. They went out and stocked up on supplies, grabbing things that they knew they'd need. Eventually there was a decent amount of fighting, to be sure, and a lot of people *did* die as things started to hit closer to home, whether by the hands of their neighbors, or by being torn apart by the things that *used* to be their neighbors.

Granted, some people *did* flee, following the grandiose notion that they could "hide things out." They went running off to the nearest mountain or lake. I don't really know what they thought they would accomplish. After all, most of them were Average Joes that lived in the suburbs, and they didn't have the first clue about surviving outside of organized society. I'm sure it may have seemed like an awesome idea at the time, but after a few days of "roughing it" set in and their cans of caviar and bottles of Dasani ran out, I imagine that the notion became a bit tiresome. They'd come limping back into town and run into a pack of deaders. I don't need to tell you what happened after that.

It was laughably stupid of them, and I have no sympathy in me.

You know what it came down to? What really allowed those of us that remained to survive the first season of the *zombie apocalypse?* Any guesses? No? Please, allow me to tell you: common fucking sense.

I know; crazy, right?

TV constantly showed us groups of haggard stragglers hiding in the woods, scrounging off the land and struggling to stay alive. They were constantly bombarded by hordes of the undead, thousands of miles away from anything even remotely resembling civilization. Taking a piss out in the middle of an open field? Seventeen zombies pop up out of nowhere just to say hello. Taking shelter in an abandoned house? Wow, there's at least three in that one room that they didn't search. Dropping a deuce in a locked bathroom stall? Silly vagabond; there's one hiding in the air duct right above your head.

Me? I still live in the same house I bought when I was twenty four, only a couple hundred miles from where the outbreak first originated. Am I sane? Well, that would be up to society to decide, if we still had a society to speak of. What I can tell you is this: never in my life have I felt so at home, so comfortable in my surroundings. The outbreak took away the laws; took away the politically correct moral perspective. I got to *be,* got to *do,* all the things that I'd ever thought about doing; thoughts that had always stayed well hidden behind the bright, plastic smile on my face that was deemed socially acceptable. Those same rules and restrictions didn't apply anymore, though.

Now, I'm an Exterminator, and God damn it, I love my work.

So, let's continue on this brief history lesson, shall we?

When shit *got real,* there were any number of issues to be overcome. Idiots tried to hoard and steal money. The ignorant bought steak. Tech geeks were uploading and downloading ... I dunno; whatever it is that tech geeks do. There was a bit of a frantic pace to it, to be sure, but most people behaved in a very civil manner given the circumstances. After all, in the early days you could never really tell who was in the early stages of infection; who would explode and attack you if you so much as looked at them the wrong way. Most of us gradually learned that if your normally docile associate randomly tried to rip your throat out, they might be infected. So we all played nice.

It was intriguing to me how polite everyone became when dealing with their fellow man under those circumstances. There were far more "pleases" and "thank yous" than I was used to hearing when I held the door open for someone. Small as it was, to me this was the first sign of remaining society drawing together.

So while the idiots were stealing money and booze, and the ignorant were buying perishable steak, I walked into the local all-purpose grocery store a mile from my house. I wasn't alone, though; it was me and my best friend- brother- Lewis. We'd known each other since grade school, and had never really strayed that far away from one another. Even now, he lived only three doors down the street from my house. I even got along with his long-time girlfriend, and that strengthened our bond. Lewis and his girlfriend would be dead within the year, but in that moment we were together, the way that siblings are supposed to be.

Ignoring everything around us, we worked our way to the rear of the store. There were only two checkout lines open, both clogged with deep lines of anxious people shuffling forward to buy what they deemed necessities. Idiots, all of them; they still thought that paper currency would matter for much longer. In contrast, our cheap plastic grocery baskets were filled with simple things that we planned to walk out the door with: aspirin, gauze, peroxide. While most people were mopping up any canned goods that they could get, we knew that these-*these*- were the true perishables. This, then, is why we made our way to the back of the store to where the pharmacy window sat.

The guy standing nervously behind the window was older than us by a couple of decades. His overcoat was white, and his hair was headed the same direction. He had a skittish look in his eyes from behind his spectacles as we approached. A scream from near the front of the store made him jump, and his eyes twitched that way for just a moment before returning to us. We then proceeded to ask him very politely for all of the amoxicillin products that he had on the shelves. The clerk informed us that he couldn't provide any of those without a prescription. I casually slipped my hand to the back of my belt as I glanced at the clerk's name tag. It read "Larry."

When possible, I always prefer to know the names of the people I kill.

"Hey, Larry?" Lewis had asked in a reasonable voice as I stood silently next to him, my knuckles curled tight around the knife hilt tucked into the back of my jeans, "You know what's happening out there, right? You've seen the news? You're obviously an educated guy. You wouldn't be the"- Lewis reached a slow hand out to tilt up Larry's nametag so that he could read the small ingrained print at the bottom- "Head Pharmacist if you weren't."

That was Lewis; always the voice of reason, and he had the silver tipped tongue of the Devil to go with it.

Larry the Pharmacist drew back from Lewis's hand looking more nervous yet, but he didn't take his eyes off of us. Lewis smiled in a disarming way. It was a smile that I'd seen a million times; It was a smile that I'd seen get him out of trouble at work; it was the smile that had led countless girls to his bed. It was a smile that never failed.

"Listen, Larry," Lewis continued, dropping his voice and leaning forward on the counter like he had a secret to tell. Body language has its own magnetism, and Larry leaned forward, too. "We aren't looking to rob you; we would never do that. We're not that type of people. We don't want everything, just what you can spare. There's way too much for us to even carry. But we're thinking long term, and we'll take whatever you can give us."

Larry seemed skeptical, and I gripped my knife tighter.

"Look," Lewis said in a soothing tone, his voice velvet smooth as he smiled that smile, "You can see what's happening outside, yeah? You can see where all of this is going?"

Larry nodded, nervous sweat beginning to bead at his hairline. Lewis- the calm, soothing, shark that he was- didn't relent in the least.

"I'm guessing that you don't have much in the way of family, am I right?" Lewis continued. The aging pharmacist shrugged in a false, disinterested manner.

"What makes you say that?" Larry asked in a sullen fashion, and- smelling blood- Lew didn't miss a beat.

"Because I've only seen three workers in this entire store, and you're one of 'em. If you had a better place to be, you'd be there. Instead,"- Lewis spread his hands wide- "you're here."

Larry didn't say anything, but I could see that Lewis had his attention. I allowed my hand to loosen from around the knife at my back. Larry didn't know it yet, but the deal had already been sealed.

"Loyalty is important," Lewis said, his voice dropping to little more than a whisper. "We respect that. Now, we have a place; a safe place. There's hellfire coming, you know it as well as we do, but our place is safe. There's a couple dozen of us, and we could use someone like you. Give us what we need and you can come with us. Stay for a few days until this blows over, or as long as you like. We've got water, food, batteries ... We're only missing one thing, and I think that one thing is you."

Lewis trailed off suggestively, but I knew that the deed was already done. I could see the wheels turning in Larry's mind as he worked things over. Local news in our area gave constant updates to the burgeoning virus in our area, and everyone except Lew and me seemed to be going a bit nuts.

"We'll need more," Larry stated, giving us a last wavering glance before he turned towards the shelves that held a countless field of bottles and vials. The pharmacist started to grab bottles of pills off of the shelves, shuffling them over to us. "Cillian based products won't be enough. We'll need anti inflammatories, bronchodilators, sedatives …"

And just like that, we had a doctor for our meager society.

Let's Meet the Players

So, let's go back to TV once more. Remember those shows that I referenced earlier? Of course you do. Who didn't make posts, send out a Tweet or a #hashtag concerning the cliffhangers that the week's episode brought?

Remember how everyone always seemed to be in the woods, or some dilapidated compound? *Everyone* was covered in filth, and you could practically smell them through your TV screen. They did their laundry in any lake or river that they could find, in the wide open wilderness, yet were always in constant fear of the deaders that were chasing them? Only the smallest part of that even stretched towards the truth.

The reality was much more mundane. Power ran out pretty quick as you can imagine. With nobody working the cranks, driving the gears, so to speak? Yeah, it was in short supply. As for being dirty? Well … I guess that kind of depended on the person. Granted, none of us could be called Lysol fresh, but we didn't look like we'd just crawled out of a garbage mound, either.

But living in the woods? Like I said earlier, a bunch of people ran to the mountains, but that had always seemed ludicrous to me. Why leave a structurally sound, fortified building to go live in the wide open woods where you could never watch every direction at once? It's damn near asinine. Our group had evaluated our options, and we'd all decided to stay in our homes. Our decision wasn't just based on the houses, though; it was about the layout of the neighborhood.

See, we lived on a cul-de-sac; typical suburban America. I had bought my corner lot house not so much that I liked it, but because it was only a handful of doors down from my family. Not that I had much in the way of family. My younger sister Lacy and her husband Francis- stupid name, but pretty good guy- had rented a house a couple plots down a few years before. My home was initially bank owned- following the always resurgent fallout of 2008- and it appealed to me because it was under market value. Meaning it was cheap.

It was a pretty big place for one person, and I tried to convince Lewis and his girl to share the space and split the cost. My best friend was open to the idea, but his girlfriend- Jasmine? Jessamyn? I really don't care- wanted a place of their own. Consequently, they rented the house across the street from my sister and Francis. The cost of the mortgage on my own didn't much matter to me, though, at least not in the end. After all, in the end, no one had a mortgage to worry about.

So.

You got me and Lewis living a few doors away from each other. Lacy and Francis across the street from Lewis. Larry, our tag a long pharmacist, actually ended up living with me. He was a bit of an odd duck; a little off kilter, so to speak. He kept mostly to himself, but it was pretty easy to see that he didn't like being alone. He'd mentioned any number of times moving into one of the empty houses along the cul-de-sac, but he never seemed to follow through. Didn't bother me much; I wasn't too fond of being alone, either.

Next you have Nancy, a widow edging into what you could call her "twilight years." She used to walk her two Scottish Terriers up and down the street at least twice a day. That is, of course, until one of them got eaten, acting as the fodder that inevitably spared Nancy her life. I don't know what purpose Nancy really served beyond whining and worrying, but- when she was sober- she helped with the cooking and the gardening. She was part of our group, and nothing mattered but the group. After that you have D'wayne (His name was Dwayne, but with his Cajun twang it sounded a bit ethnic.) He was a retired air conditioning repair man, and lived next door to me. His accent made him a little hard to understand at times, but I don't think that there is anything in this world that he couldn't fix or build. His wife's name was Cecille, and she was as equally pointless as Nancy. Sweet woman, though.

Sister Tracy: now this is one tough, hard-nosed bitch. She'd been retired from the habit for God knows how long, but she still had that natural air of disdainful wrath and Catholic guilt. She had to be pushing seventy, but in the early days I'd personally seen her fight off two deaders by herself with nothing more than a garden hoe, hacking away at them with divine ferocity until they were nothing more than twitching mounds. The sister had a heavy voice in our meager council when we made decisions. She and Lewis got along great, but she had a cold eye for me. We were cordial to one another-worked together as a team- but that was the best that could be said. She always got a bit frosty when I was about, almost like she could sense how much I loved my job, my position in our community. It was like she could sense that I was a bit off, skipping outside of the careful boundaries laid out by the Lord.

But hey, the Lord wasn't here, was he? Or maybe he was, and this had been his plan all along. Maybe he finally got fed up watching his creation destroy themselves; watching us wrench and rape each other physically and morally, flogging and murdering, pillaging and burning. Maybe that almighty being just got tired of it all, and remembered an old story- told so long ago- about a believer, a boat, and a flood …

Nah, I'm just kidding. I've never had any reason to give a shit about any of the spiritual stuff that people seem to cling so hard to. I've always seen organized religion as the most well-structured business in the world; kudos to them. And the Bible thumpers? Even worse.

Let's be clear. I've known that there was something off inside of me since I was a child, but even I can't wrap my head around the hypocrisies of the Bible; it's nothing but words written on a page by a plain ol' Joe, and interpreted anyway that the reader wants. *That* is the word of the Lord.

But here's what's real, and this is fact: we didn't survive by the will of God. We didn't survive by some fluke chance. We survived because we banded together, using that magical adhesive- *dah-dahn-da-duh!*- common sense.

Now, for full disclosure, I had to kill more than a handful along our street that had turned, but in my own defense I did it as mercifully as possible, doing my very best to ignore the sense of burgeoning freedom in my belly. Once they were taken care of- and when it came to the actual deed, they all became nameless faces- Lewis and I got to talking, with Francis chiming in. It all seemed very, very clear to us:

The world was in accelerating chaos; order had fallen; the dead were walking the earth.

*... thought ... thought ... though*t ...

... and we lived in a cul-de-sac surrounded by eight foot high cinder block walls with only one route of access.

Well, we built a wall out of anything that we could find- and there was plenty; in the early days aspirin wasn't the only thing that most people didn't think to grab- right across the entry to our street. D'wayne engineered it and directed us, and by the time our gate was done it was probably more formidable than the cinder blocks that encircled the rest of the street. The sturdy gate was ten feet high, hinged at the wall so that we could open it when we needed to, and reinforced in every possible way. We'd even run supported platforms across the length of the cinderblock walls so that whoever was on watch would have an easier time patrolling the street. Just like that, *boom*: secured compound.

The next thing we did- well, to be honest, the next thing we did was kill off a neighboring street where everyone had turned- was establish our hierarchy. You can't have animals in the wild- and believe me, in our own way we were animals; we had to be- without a hierarchy. It didn't take a genius to figure out the roles that we were all going to play.

As in the wild, genetics and personality decided who stood in what position. It was a lot like our disbanded government, except that in our society everyone's vote mattered. No matter the station, no matter the purpose, we talked and worked our way to a consensus. It didn't matter if you were silver tongued Lewis speaking with worthless Nancy; your opinion mattered. If you were Wife of God Sister Tracy talking with me; your opinion mattered. It was never a long debate. Everything was terse and quick because- especially in the early days- it had to be. We'd reach a consensus, and then we'd move on.

The next obstacle that came up was self-supportive food. Now, thanks to Larry, Lewis, and me, we had enough antibiotics to last us for years. But vitamins wouldn't keep your belly full. My sister Lacy was actually the one to come up with the idea to turn all of the front yards into garden patches. Personally, I didn't know the first thing about gardening, but thanks to a couple dozen packs of seeds pilfered from a nearby dollar store, by the time our perishable food stuffs started running out we had several yards growing with corn. Sure, we had patches of tomatoes and potatoes, but mostly it was corn.

Sound too mundane and simple? That's only because you don't realize how much you can do with corn. Don't take it personally; neither did I. Lacy did, though. Corn, apparently, has a thousand different uses in every different culture- bread, masa, tortillas- and my sister knew almost all of them. And then, once the corn had been shucked from the cob, we had something to wipe our asses with. The true genius, though, came from Francis.

Now, I need you to understand my brother in law; see him very clearly, if you will. Francis was a good ol' boy, rotund and ornery. He chewed tobacci' until it ran out, and then he figured out how to grow his own. He hated niggers, and was still a die-hard fan of the now defunct Florida State University Football team. *Hail, 'Noles!* But for all of his rough neck demeanor, Francis had a thinking man's mind combined with good ol' hillbilly perspective. You know what he showed us how to do with batches of Lacy's corn?

How to brew moonshine the old fashioned way.

Now, I know how weak that might sound. Most of the survivors in Southern Nevada would have either derided us- or killed us- for a sip of that clear brew. It was never about the alcohol, though, (although, admittedly, we all indulged in a few sips here and there); it was that, when burned down enough, moonshine could be used as a rough form of fuel for vehicles. So all those movies of survivors straggling through desolation on foot? Yeah, those weren't true, either. We still had several cars on our street, and Francis's moonshine is what fueled them when we decided to take them out.

What about gasoline? I'd imagine that you're asking right now. *Why not just siphon some out from all of the abandoned cars and put them into your own? I mean, it seems so simple; that's how they did it on TV.*

Yeah, that is how they did it on TV. They did a lot of things on TV. Doesn't necessarily make it right, though. I'll tell you why in a moment. Just shut up and be patient.

Now, provided that we could find the keys, we basically had the pick of any vehicle that we wanted. Not that we really had to search them out, though; there were ample cars on our street. With our homemade fuel they never went as fast as they were built to, but it was a fair spot better than walking. The short coming to Francis's hooch was that it took time to brew, and the engines burned through it pretty quick.

As to why didn't we siphon fuel? Well, we could have and we did. The reality was that one gallon of gas doesn't get you as far as you'd expect, and lugging twenty gallons of it a dozen miles is a harrowing endeavor. It's no fun, trust me. Moreover, gas that sits in the tank for too long grows stagnant, and will clog and eat out the hoses and engines, which caused more of a problem than it was worth. Not only were we stranded, but we lost the vehicle, too. If we went out it was generally on foot, and if we had to use a vehicle, it ran on Francis's moonshine.

Now, there's only one thing missing from this picture I've painted so far, and any parent out there will know what it is: children. I won't go into the details of the how or why. I love that in this broken down world I can basically give in to my primal instincts and kill with a smile on my lips, but I've always had a soft spot for kids. Our street started out with eight; we were down to three, two girls and a boy. Their parents were Shawn and Deidre, and they had been two that I'd had to put down in the first few days after "the first case" was reported in our area. Everyone on the street acted as surrogate parents to them, but they lived with Lacy and Francis.

I'd die before I let anything happen to those kids. They loved my sister, and adored Francis like a favorite eccentric uncle, but for the most part they were beyond wary with me, especially the younger two. I have a hard time understanding why. I'd saved them, after all, killing their parents before their parents could kill them. It wasn't my fault that they were in the room when I did it.

They would understand when they were older.

Zombie 101

Lesson #1:

Now, I'm sure you're already sick of hearing about it, but let's skip back to the falsity of television once more. Why am I telling you about it if it's redundant? Because I can't stress enough that knowing the difference between TV and reality is what will keep you alive.

Recall the heroic, stalwart survivors in our favorite flicks and episodes. They fought off ravening hordes at least once a week, and were always under constant threat of being overrun. Hell, they couldn't take a piss in the middle of a wide open field without at least one popping up out of nowhere. I'm not judging; I was just as intrigued as everyone else.

Every single person was a crack shot, wielding guns that never seemed to run out of ammo unless the plot line demanded it. But shit, every twelve year old could put a .45 slug through the eye of a deader at thirty yards … blindfolded. ..with one hand tied behind their back. In the event that the bullets did run out, our heroes could walk forward with their trusty Swiss Army knife and shove it easily through a deader's skull, dropping it lifelessly to the ground.

Living in the midst of everything, I have to laugh at humanity's thought process. Just for a quick anatomy lesson, the human femur is stronger than concrete, and next to the spur of the elbow and the enamel on your teeth, the cranium is the hardest part of the body. Of course, fiction is always more enjoyable and easier to create when you haven't had to live through reality. To be honest, fiction is much more exciting.

Deaders are pretty quick; that's the first thing that you need to know. Sure, they aren't the most graceful things in the world, but they can get some speed behind them when they choose to. They don't have much of a thought process outside of sheer instinct: Kill; eat. Not necessarily in that order. They don't work as a team or as a pack. They just happen to frequently move together in groups, almost like some part of them remembers what it was like to socialize.

Remember the old episodes of *Shark Week* on the Discovery channel? Where some scientist or another would chum the water and then throw in a half torn tuna? The sharks would converge on it. There could be dozens in the water, but they didn't work together; they just attacked. Deaders are the same way; all muscle, no mind.

Now, you can kill them pretty easy with a gun; they die as efficiently as we do when half of their head gets blown off. Bullets are a precious commodity that we held onto for ourselves as best we could, though. Ammo was hard to get before the virus took hold- thanks in large part to our now dead President- and it was even harder, now. Fortunately for us, our street had a tidy little supply sourced together from our own people. Francis- hillbilly 'Merican and staunch supporter of the Second Amendment- had a nice selection for a variety of different handguns and rifles with plenty of rounds to match each. I had my Sig 9mm with a couple of cases of ammunition. Lewis and D'wayne each had a number of rifles and shotguns for hunting. Hell, even Sister Tracy had a little Derringer that she'd kept tucked away. It was a veritable fortune in current day value, but- needless to say- they were for an absolutely last resort.

Our day to day "tools" were of a rougher sort, but possibly more effective. See, despite what television would have you think, people can miss when they fire a gun. *Especially* when they're scared, or have the shaky hands of their fight or flight mechanism kicking in. It's a little harder to miss with a good ol' fashioned Louisville slugger, though, and a good solid swing does about the same amount of damage as a bullet.

See, TV almost had it right on that account. Almost. What TV never did was explain and validate the simple underlying fact that deaders don't feel pain; they don't feel anything. You, as the viewer, were supposed to infer it, but the broader picture was never given to you. You can crack them across the ribs with a pipe, shoot them in the arm, stab them in the chest. They might move at the impact, but they didn't *feel* their ribs breaking, the flesh shriveling away from the entry sight of a gunshot wound, their punctured lungs filling with blood. But, yeah, smashing their head apart seemed to do the trick.

Personally, I've had enough practice at putting them down that I can generally get the job done with one shot, but I prefer to use three.(Firstly, because it's prudent; secondly, because I like it.) What the average viewer would never understand, though, is that hitting an angry deader in the head for a clean kill shot is harder than you would think. Physics plays a huge role, and human error takes care of the rest. Deaders aren't stationary targets, and most people are scared when they find themselves in a face to face situation. Moreover, the skull is like a bobble head figurine; it will swivel and bounce around. Blows can easily glance off, allowing injury, but dispersing the force of impact.

What I found in the first few days was that the knee, hip or ankle was the first place I wanted to hit. It didn't matter whether they felt pain or not; you break apart an articulating, weight bearing joint and they fell to the ground like a grumpy sack of bloody oatmeal. The fact that they didn't feel anything was actually an asset to us in that sense because they didn't know to try and compensate for the injury. They wouldn't shift their weight to another leg and hobble after us; no, they'd just flop around on the ground, attempting to crawl forward, and we could decide whether to flee to safety or kill them. I generally preferred the latter, although I'm not above admitting that I've had to back off more than once. Common sense, remember?

Lesson #2:

The next thing that you need to know is that deaders are disgusting. They're not just the rotten, torn, desiccated corpses you saw on the boob tube. No, they're covered in festering sores and open, puss filled wounds, any one of which could infect you. Like Herpes. It's not just the act of being bitten that can infect you; a scratch can do it, or sometimes-depending on the number of sores they have- a simple touch of their tepid, slimy skin to yours.

Simple precaution? Wear clothing. I know it sounds too easy to be legitimate, but it works. Socks, shoes, jeans, a long sleeved shirt … They can bite and claw at you as much as they want, but if it doesn't *touch* your body- if there's a layer of protection between their teeth and your skin- you're pretty much okay. Sound stupid? Give it a shot. Go get a pair of Levi's and try to bite through them. Let's see what rips first: the denim, or your teeth. Granted, it wasn't always pleasant. It can get pretty warm in our section of Vegas, but it's a far cry better than the alternative.

Now, remember how I said they move in packs? Depending on where you're located, the packs can get big; very big. *Thousands,* big. Simple solution?

Stay away from the fucking packs!

Seriously, these things aren't T-1000 thinking machine Terminators. Don't get in their line of sight, don't give them a reason to notice you, and they'll never know you're there. It's really that simple. If it's a smaller pack- maybe a dozen or so?- I've found that moving in a circle works well.

I generally advise my people to go the other way, but if you ever find yourself in a jam that you can't get out of (or in my case, don't want to) kill them while moving backwards in a circular pattern. They're quick, but the stupid things will just follow you like a line of ants. Make sure you always know where the lead one is, but your focal point should be on the stragglers. As you circle around you'll draw closer to those at the tail end of the pack, and since the shortest distance between two points is a straight line those are the ones that will attack you, mostly one by one. As long as you stay on your toes and have your wits about you, you can basically pick them off one at a time and make it out in one piece.

Lesson #3:

Accept the fact that deaders are stronger than you, by a lot. They're not some cookie cutter monsters thought up by George Romero or M. Night Shyamalan. Every single one of them is different. If they were fast runners when they were alive, they're fast as a deader. If they were bodybuilders or powerlifters when they were alive, then they're strong as a deader. If they were six foot eight when they were alive, then *they're still six foot fucking eight as a deader.* Get the picture?

But here's the irony: even if someone was small or frail when they were alive, they're still probably stronger than you as a deader. To my reckoning, the reason is pretty simple.

The human body is a brilliant machine, and it uses pain as a warning sign. If you were to go to the gym and attempt to lift a weight that your body couldn't handle, you'd feel pain. In your joints, in your tendons, in your back, in the individual fascia that make up your muscles. It's not that you can't get the weight up; it's that your body is using pain to subliminally tell you that- if you continue- you're liable to tear a bicep, herniate a disk, or separate a tendon or ligament from the bone. Pain is your body's way of trying to protect you from harming yourself.

Deaders don't have that restriction. They don't feel pain, they can't recognize the warning signs of their body threatening to rip apart, and can mindlessly push themselves beyond the physical limits that any living person has. They don't care if they dislocate a shoulder while slamming someone twice their size to the ground; they don't care if they tear every tendon in their hand while ripping your knee from its socket. *They don't feel it.*

I guess the moral of the story is this: size matters, and in the land of this broken America, deaders are giants. Never, *ever,* try to go hand to hand with them.

The First Time

Everyone has a "my first time" story, am I right? It generally starts out along the lines of : "In high school we were going steady for three months. He/ she was nervous, I was afraid, but I just loved him/ her so much that I knew I was ready."

We have a different sort of "first time" story, now. In this glorious, shattered land, when you hear someone talking about their first time it's about the first deader that they put down. Some people are proud of it; some say it with a halting guilt. Some won't talk about it at all. It's been long enough that many of us have turned into a bunch of whores, and I can count the virgins I've met on one hand.

My first time? I still sigh in reflection when I think about it. It was a pretty glorious, triumphant day. After all, how many people ever get to kill the first person to break their heart?

Everyone, at some point in time, has a first love. Whether you were dating, whether it was unrequited, whether you were dumped, or the one to do the dumping and realized that you made a mistake afterward. I had one the same way that you, Late Night Buyer, yourself did. Out of respect for the dead, let's call mine … Pat.

Now, Pat broke my heart. We were in love, or at least I thought we were. Pat had made me feel normal, and had spawned feelings in me that I'd never felt. I spent the better part of my formative dating years with Pat. We never had sex, although I'd wanted us to. No, Pat split things off, saying that we should "just be friends" … and then went out and began banging one of my closest acquaintances.

I grew up, grew older, and –as most of us do- outgrew that whimsical first love. Never got rid of the resentment, but outgrew it. You can imagine how shocked I was when the outbreak first hit my cul-de-sac and I saw Pat stumbling mindlessly down the street. It was a fluke and nothing more that Pat and I, after years of separation, had ended up living in the same neighborhood. But Pat was right there, stumbling and snarling; killing one of Nancy's black Scottish terriers as the old lady herself tried to pull the other one to safety.

There hadn't been much time to think; there never was. This was in the early days, back before we had erected our wall to cut us off from the outside. Not that I really gave it a lot of thought. In that moment, that wonderful, glorious moment, everything made sense. Something clicked for me, and I grabbed the first thing close to hand as I headed out my front door: an aluminum softball bat that was leaning in the corner.

The sound of the bat cracking across Pat's jaw was amazing, resounding with a ringing *ping* like a bell that had been tolled. The Scottish terrier that had been dangling from Pat's mouth had still been alive, thrashing weakly, but my bat ended that. I considered it a mercy killing, while Nancy- stupid, doe eyed bitch- continued to stand there and scream instead of running away. Pat was still alive, though, at least as much as any of these things can be said to still be alive.

Pat's left cheekbone had been crushed into bloody effluence, but the rest of the deader's body seemed to be moving just right. So I hit it again. And again … and again. I hit Pat with my aluminum bat until my arms were too tired to swing anymore. Nancy and her last Scottie continued to yap in the background the entire time. When it was done, Pat wasn't much more than a lumpy mess on the sidewalk. I was breathing hard, my heart was pounding in my chest, but my hands were steady as I turned to Nancy and very calmly told her that she should probably go home. The woman nodded in a numb fashion, strands of hair that had come loose from her gray bun flapping around her face.

I stood evaluating the splattered mess before me. I needed to talk to Lewis. It was official; the outbreak had reached our neighborhood. Things had "hit home," as they say, and we needed to work out how we were going to handle it. I figured I'd better give Lacy a call, too (the phones were still working back then.) First though, there was something else I had to do.

I walked back to my house and exchanged the bloody bat for a flat edged shovel before then heading back over to the twitching mass that was leaking its way down the gutter. I held the shovel in one hand while dragging a large rolling trash can behind me. I couldn't just leave something like this lying around; there were kids about, after all.

Welcome to Branberry Street; we're the little cul de sac at the end of the world.

"You're doing it again," Lacy said from where she paced next to me. Her head was a few feet below me, and she had to tilt her head up to look at me. It was perfectly natural, considering that I was walking across the top of the brick wall that ringed Branberry. My bat dangled absently in my hand, bouncing and clanging against the lip of the wall as I turned my gaze towards my sister. Avery- eldest of the three siblings that lived with my sister- walked at her heels, not making eye contact with me anytime I glanced her way.

"Doing what?" I asked absently, allowing the bat to *ping* against the wall with each step that I took. We'd erected a platform around the perimeter of the wall for people to move across if there was a need, but I was walking the narrow width of the block wall. I'd done it so many times that it was easy, barely more than a thought, but the potential ten foot fall on either side of me was liable to be the biggest rush I got today. My rushes- my brush with feeling alive- were becoming harder and harder to come by.

"Trying to find a deader," Lacy responded, reaching an absent hand out towards Avery. The little preteen took the bait, and clasped my sister's palm easily enough, but kept her eyes on the ground while I was looking their direction. I'd found that I was starting to grow irritated with the way that Avery and her younger siblings wouldn't look at me. It was frustrating mainly because I'd done them a *solid* when I'd rescued them. I cared about all three of those kids in my own little way, and none of them seemed to appreciate it. I didn't respond to Lacy as I continued my patrol, but that didn't slow her in the least. I cared about my sister, but she'd never known when to let something go.

"How many days has it been?" she asked, looking up at me with her eyes crinkled against the glare of the sun. She'd always been a stubborn one, never knowing when to stop. I wasn't going to answer her, but then figured, what was the harm?

"Four," I said.

Lacy didn't respond, but continued to trail me, the despondent Avery following in her footsteps. My sister weaved around a yellow fire hydrant that stood like a silent sentinel in the sidewalk; a sentinel that was useless, worthless, and couldn't help us even if it wanted to. It was nothing but a fallen monument to a fallen civilization.

"Have you talked with Lewis?" Lacy asked a couple yards later, flipping her ponytail over her shoulder. At the age of twenty five, the ponytail was one of the few things that Lacy had kept since childhood.

"Lew doesn't tell me what I can and can't do," I replied. It was true; Lewis was my best friend, but in this broken world we had very different views on what was best for Branberry. When we had decided to fortify our street, I'd let him to take the lead. Lew was pragmatic, while I'd always loved living in the moment. He'd had goals and objectives, while my view point had been much simpler.

Lewis had felt that we should stay holed up, venturing out only if we needed to, and keeping to ourselves. I had wanted to bring in as many people as we could to our little street; bring in as many of the stragglers that roamed beyond the safety of our walls. It's not like we didn't have room to spare. This was one area where Sister Tracy and I had agreed.

Plus, there was also the matter of my growing … needs; Needs that most in our meager group had started to recognize. I can't say that everyone approved, but most respected it. My *needs* had kept them safe and they knew it.

In the end, we'd all reached a compromise. I'd gone out on my own and cleared out the homes on the neighboring street. I was very careful, very thorough, and it took me the better part of the day. Don't misconstrue, though; I enjoyed every second of it. At the end of that day our pact was honored: Any survivors that we found could stay there for as long as they wanted. Whether it was for the night, the week, or for the long haul, it didn't matter. We'd found any number in those first couple of months, and- if deemed worthy- we brought them back to their new homes. The other street was doing very well, now, thank you very much.

But right now, in this moment, we were on *my* street.

I hopped off the wall, pivoting in the air at the last second to grab the lip of the walkway and break my plummeting descent. My sneakers landing with a slight scuffing sound. I was well aware that there was a time and place for heavy boots, but sneakers served all purposes and were better suited for speed when it was needed. My current sneakers were expensive, the type that I could never have afforded before the outbreak. But wouldn't you know it? Some of the shoes from Avery's parent's closet fit me perfectly. Score!

"I know that," Lacy said as I landed on the ground, drawing me out of my reverie and reminding me that we'd been in the midst of conversation. She seemed at a loss for words- which was unusual for her- and pulled a crumpled plastic water bottle from her back pocket to take a swig. The old, thin plastic was crinkled and almost formless, but it still served a purpose. I'd never had any use for it before, but the term "recycling" had a helluva lot more value to it now. We had to make do with what we had at our disposal. Lacy offered the bottle to Avery, and the little preteen let her hand go to gulp at it. I watched as the little girl swigged, noting that she had a habit of backwashing into the bottle. Gross. While she engrossed herself in hydration, I took a moment to observe her.

Avery had been holding her brother and sister- Troy and Bree, respectively- crumpled against the wall with her arms curled protectively about them as I'd put Shawn and Diedre down. I'd used my bat, of course, the way that I always did if I could. The bat was effective, but not very glamorous. I'd been focused on the two deaders in front of me, but I'd still caught glimpses of the three children huddled in the corner.

Troy- four- and Bree- seven- had been wailing and shrieking so loudly that their eyes were squeezed shut. They would have bolted any direction that they could go if it hadn't been for the arms of their "Big

Sissy" curled around them. Avery had been screaming too, but her eyes had been wide open. She had watched me put her parents down with nothing more than a blank expression on her face. She had been the only one of the three to actually witness what I had done. If any of them truly had a reason to hate me, it was her.

That's why I was surprised when she looked up at me, shifting bangs that had grown too long and dangled in her eyes, out of her face.

"Why do you do it?" she asked in a flat voice. It wasn't the question that caught me off guard; it was the way that she asked it. There was no judgment in her tone; it was a truly honest question. I wasn't used to her speaking to me directly, though, so it took me a moment to respond. The socially acceptable answers and reasons- all of which I knew by heart- were too many to count. I opted to go with the best response: the one that was mostly the truth. I always tried to be truthful. After all, out here? What was the point of lying?

"Because it keeps you safe," I said, looking her in the eyes. "It keeps everyone safe."

Avery didn't budge or bat a lash as she took another swig- and another backwash- from the crumpled bottle of water.

"Do you like it?" she asked.

I didn't have to think about it this time. Like I said; why lie?

"Yes. I like it a lot."

"Why don't you just use your gun? It would be easier, wouldn't it?"

"Probably," I said, opting not to tell her that I took a greater pleasure from getting up close and personal with my bat. "But guns make too much noise. We don't want to do anything to draw their attention to Branberry. If they don't know we're here, then they just walk on by when they happen to come our way. We have to be careful to make sure that they don't know where we are. That's why we don't use the guns."

Avery considered this for a moment in silence, and then held the crumpled water bottle out to me, offering a sip. I thought about her backwash; that thin, invisible layer of filth that I could almost imagine I could see swirling through the clear water that we filtered ourselves. *Eh, why not?* I thought to myself. While I'd never been a fan of the "five second" rule, I considered myself to be utterly pragmatic. *God made dirt, and dirt don't hurt, right?*

I took the offered bottle with my free hand and raised it to my lips. Yeah; I could taste her spit. I'd just finished the single swallow I could force down when Avery said "Can I come with you?"

Lacy and I both said "no" at the same time, but I'd imagine that it was for much different reasons. Avery looked pouty and crestfallen, but she didn't object, although I did notice that from beneath the overhang of her bangs she had a considering look in her eye.

Lacy looked at me, and I could see her emotions warring on her face. Next to Sister Tracy, Lacy probably objected more than anyone else to what it was that I did. But she was also my kid sister. She loved me, looked up to me- I don't know why- and understood that I had to do it. I needed it.

"We're out of zip ties," she said, sounding half disgusted with the admission. Her eyes tilted incrementally away from me, not meeting my gaze. Avery was watching me, though. My ears perked up.

"Yeah?" I said, trying to suppress the sudden eagerness in my voice. "D'wayne had a full case just a couple of weeks ago."

"No," my sister said with a shake of her head. "They're the wrong size. We need to tie up the fence posts for the animals, and I need the big ones."

Lacy was referring the big backyard of the vacant house where we kept our "livestock." We didn't live anywhere near a farm, so we had scrounged up anything that we could find or trap. Exotic pet shops had been a boon in the early days; no one had been thinking about bringing home a new puppy when the outbreak hit our area. Consequently, we had gathered up a little den of tasty, edible creatures that we used to sustain ourselves. The fad of "mini pigs" in particular had proven fruitful, but we also had coyotes, snakes, and even a big horned sheep that Francis had brought back. Don't ask me how he got it.

Lacy's request might have been a legitimate need, or maybe she was just trying to give me a reprieve. Next to water/ shelter/ food/ medicine, zip ties, duct tape and superglue were some of the most important things that we used. After all, if you can't fix something with any of those, you have a hell of a problem.

"Just do me a favor," Lacy continued. "Bring Frankie with you; he's itching to get out."

I gave her a nod that was little more than a cursory afterthought. I'd already started to walk away, twirling my bat in my hand. Lacy called out after me.

"But talk to Lewis first!"

"Absolutely not," Lewis said, looking up at me from where he and D'wayne- the retired mechanic- were tinkering beneath the hood of one of the cars that we used to drive around our vicinity. Francis's moonshine worked, but it seemed like it had a tendency to eat away at some of the more delicate parts of the engines and hoses.

I didn't even bother to respond, and looked Lewis blandly in the eye. My silence was its own answer. Lewis pushed himself away from the hood, wiping his blackened hands off on his not so clean jeans.

"I need you here," he said firmly. He said it in a voice that was meant to carry, and had all the authority of a middle manager wrangling his employees. I knew him better than that, though. It was a big show for anyone that might have been listening, but he and I both knew that I was going to do whatever the hell I wanted to do. While the boundaries may have withered away over the last year or so, I had always lived by my own set of rules and guidelines. That's what had always made Lew and me an unlikely couple of friends; we were complete opposites in many ways. Even before puberty, Lew had always been a study in cool, calculated thought; I'd always been more inclined to rapid action.

I crossed my arms over my chest, continuing to say nothing as I stared him blandly in the eye. He could play the tough, stalwart leader as much as he wanted, but he wasn't fooling me. I knew him too well for that.

"It's safer if you're here," Lew said, and then his voice dropped down a bit. "Everyone feels better if you're here."

Oh, you sweet little shit, I thought to myself, *look at you trying to cater to my ego.*

I opted not to say anything- letting silence be my answer once more- and cocked my head suggestively. I wasn't about to back down, and Lew got a stubborn look to his face. Things could have gotten a little more confrontational- and it wouldn't have been the first time- if D'wayne hadn't broken the silence for us.

"Ac'chilly," the mechanic said in his Cajun twang as he pushed himself from beneath the undercarriage of the car, "I could use a few things m'self; if yer gonna make a run, dat is."

D'wayne looked up at Lewis, and there were dark oil stains tinting his salt and pepper beard. Lewis gave him a bland, somewhat betrayed look, but then finally relented. "Give me a second?" he asked, looking at me. I knew what he meant. He wasn't asking for privacy; he was telling me that we had to speak for a moment. I shrugged with feigned indifference, and turned around to stroll off a few feet. I felt the weight of Lew's thin arm drape itself around my shoulder as he walked me off to the curb.

"You gotta stop doing this," Lew hissed, dropping the mantle of "wise leader" and becoming the guy that I grew up with. He kept his voice low, and said it next to my ear. He had to bend his neck, since he had a half a foot of height on me. "It was all good in the beginning; we needed it. But now? Now, you're just getting fucking dangerous."

I couldn't- in all honesty- disagree with him. Lew, more than any of the others, knew how much my needs had blossomed. It had all been fun and games when we were kids. Playing guns, cops and robbers, cowboys and Indians … fun little things that were heavily steeped in violence. Those were always my favorite games. But now, in this reality? Well, I guess that most people would have drawn back at those fantasies coming to life, but I'd embraced it. Money talks, and bull shit walks, as they say.

"I know what I'm doing," I told him in the same lowered voice. "It's perfectly safe. I've been over the area a thousand times. Shit, it's been over a week since we've even seen one."

"Four days," Lew said, his whispered voice still managing to crack like a whip as he called me out on my lie. "I watched you go over the wall four days ago, and you weren't back until the sun was starting to go down." He cast a quick glance over his shoulder to where D'wayne was still tinkering with the car engine before looking back to me. "I know exactly what the fuck you were doing. You fucking stupid?"

"I put down three," I said without a hint of shame or remorse. Lew was blustering, and I knew it. You'd think- after all the years we'd known each other- that he would realize he couldn't fool me with bravado. "They were moving like drones and heading our direction. I got to them before they got to us. You're welcome."

Lewis didn't respond, but his lips tightened in a way that I knew well. I spoke up before he could lecture me.

"I gotta get out, Lew," I said beneath my voice, allowing some of my need to leak out. "I gotta *do* something. I can't stand sitting still. I need to move. I need to have a purpose. You know how it is, right? How many times a day are you jerking off, now?"

I was the only one that knew that Lewis's longtime girlfriend was actually a lesbian. He'd taken the revelation hard but the two of them maintained pretenses, although I secretly thought that- Jesabelle? Jermaine?- had taken up with Sister Tracy. All those late night prayer sessions, and you know how those Catholics can be.

At my words, my best friend recoiled like he'd been slapped. His face contorted with cold rage, and I took a second to enjoy the fact that I'd managed to get under his skin. Lew would have pistol whipped anyone else that insulted him like that, but aside from letting his arm fall from my shoulder he didn't do anything to me. I don't know if was because of our sibling like relationship, or if because he knew that if he brought a fight to me- *hey Silly Sally, if you want to dally-* I'd be more than willing to give one right back. After all, sibling fights are *always* the best fights. Nothing compliments love better than a healthy dose of hate.

"Fuck off," he said, a hint of the old fire remaining in his eyes. *There it is,* I thought to myself. I managed to keep my face straight, but was smiling on the inside. *This* was the guy that I'd grown up with. *This* was the real Lewis, who didn't feel the need for pretense because the weight of leadership hung heavy on his shoulders.

"I have to move, man," I said, relenting with a sigh as I rubbed at my temples. I could feel the pressure there, building and growing as my need- my addiction- called to me. "There're things I have to do."

Lew didn't respond immediately, and I could see that he was pissed at me. Good. Anger is *truth,* and while it may be ill mannered, it never tells a lie.

"You're not going alone," he said stiffly, relenting. "Who's going with you?"

"Frankie," I said immediately, feeling my shoulders unbunch as a flood of eager adrenaline coursed through me. "Lacy told me that he wants to get out for a bit."

"Fuckin' Frankie," Lew said with a shake of his head. "I don't know which one of the two of you is more of a pain in my ass."

I allowed myself to smile as I held my hand up to him, cocked at the elbow. "Trust me?" I asked, even though I knew I didn't need to. Lew sighed in vexation, but he slapped his palm into mine a moment later and we did one of those weird little "bro hugs" that involved a lot of slapping on the back.

"Yeah," Lew said as we mutually separated. "I fuckin' trust you. But get a list. Just check around, see who needs what, and check on Nancy, would ya? She's starting to get a bit emotional, again. Shit, I thought that she'd be done with menopause by now. See if she needs anything?" *Absolutely fucking not,* I thought to myself.

"Sure," I said out loud as I turned to walk away. I would honor the agreement, and planned to return and talk to D'wayne in a few minutes, but for right now I had to leave. I didn't want to give Lew a chance to reconsider things. I was going on a vacation, and I wasn't going to give him a chance to second guess it. I'd gotten maybe a dozen yards down the road when Lewis hollered out to me.

"And tell Frankie not to bring that fuckin' crossbow!"

I closed the front door to Lacy's (formerly) beautiful two story home as quietly as I could and stepped inside. The latch made little more than a soft, muted click, but I waited.

One … two … thr- …

"Cletus!" Frankie hollered from upstairs, his hollow voice barreling down the stairwell. He'd always called me Cletus, and I'd never really known why. Of course, I'd never really bothered to ask, either. Cletus worked for me, and there was a certain sardonic humor in it, as well. I heard a rapid series of heavy, rhythmic thumps- like an overeager golden retriever falling down the stairs- as Frankie bounded down the stairs of the home that he and my sister shared. "Look at this shit!" he bellowed as an introduction.

Frankie rounded the corner of the stairwell, leaping down the last few steps with childlike enthusiasm. If you took me out of the equation, I think that Frankie was probably the most content of our little group with the way that the world was lived. He lived in the moment- maybe even more than I did- and loved nothing better than what he called "redneck good times." This could be anything from killing deaders to making homemade explosives, to seeing how fast he could clean all of his rifles, to seeing how many pairs of my sister's underwear he could put on over his jeans- one faded set over the other- before she finally snapped and started screaming at him.

I liked Frankie.

As he came into my field of view I saw that my hillbilly brother-inlaw had a crossbow in his hands. I knew for a fact that Frankie loved that crossbow with the type of fondness that most people reserve for a well behaved child. Maybe the same way that I loved my bat.

As always, there was a prodigious lump at his lower lip where he kept a constant plug of his home grown chewin' tabbaci'. While Lacy had been growing corn and other vegetables, Frankie had somehow found the seeds to cultivate his own strand of coarse tobacco leaves. It was all natural, and his teeth had taken on an unhealthy brown sheen within the last half year.

"Check it out," he said by way of introduction, holding the crossbow out to me like a proud father offering up his newborn for familial inspection. "I cut down on the draw line. It's a bitch to pull, but I bet I can get an extra thirty or forty feet on the distance."

I made some grunts that sounded appreciative and intrigued, but I honestly could have cared less. Frankie liked killing deaders almost as much as I did, but he grew up hunting game, and preferred to do it like any true hunter: from a distance. Personally, I liked to be a little bit closer when I put them down.

"What are your plans for the day?" I asked, already knowing what the answer would be. Frankie gave me a feigned look, like I'd just asked him the most idiotic question in the world, but his face split into a wide grin.

"Ah, hell, Cleet; the same as they are every day," he said, pausing to spit a stream of brown saliva into a dingy cup that sat on the kitchen counter. "Find somethin' to do, take a nap when I get bored. Might find somethin' else to do after that. I'm feeling 'specially ambitious today, so after Lacy starts clamoring at me about nothin', I might just take *another* nap before it's bed time."

I smiled. I'd always liked Frankie's sense of humor. It was raw and natural, and there were times that I wished I could emulate it. He and I got along well. Sometimes better than Lacy and I did. Most times, maybe.

"I'm heading out for a bit," I said. "You feel like making a run?"

Frankie's mood changed in an instant. His eyes snapped up and his face went blank before focusing to a needle's point. His affable grin came back pretty quick, though.

"*Fuck* yeah, I feel like making a run," he said, smiling wide. "You check it out with Lewis, first?"

Jesus; seriously? I thought to myself, resisting the urge to roll my eyes. *Why does everyone think I need his permission to do something?*

"Lew's good with it," I said. "He's counting on you to keep me out of trouble. I told him you could." I gave Frankie a suggestive look that was half devilish and half baiting. "You *can* keep me out of trouble, right?"

"Hell no!" Frankie laughed, without a care in the world. "Why would I want to? Getting into trouble is half the fun!"

Like I said; I liked Frankie.

"Lemme grab a few things real quick," he continued, setting the crossbow on the counter as he pulled his duffel from the closet. The backpack was worn, military green, and a holdover souvenir from the time he'd spent enlisted in the USMC. Frankie grabbed a couple bottles of water and some meat that he, himself, had dehydrated into jerky. I hesitated to ask where it came from or what animal it was. It was meat, and it served its purpose. He shoved everything into the duffel, and then reached for a quiver of short arrows that sat on the kitchen table.

"Lew said not to bring the crossbow," I said. I could have let it go; I could have said nothing at all. It's not like Frankie would listen to me, anyway. But this was my own little way of egging on the situation, and I knew exactly how Frankie would respond. He was always good as a source for entertainment.

"Lewis don't know shit," Frankie muttered, half to himself. "Suzanna goes where I go."

"You shot Jordan, last time," I jibed, bringing it up on purpose. Jordan was a black guy that lived just beyond the wall to Branberry. He'd lived there for years, and while he was one of the few on the block that had managed to survive the outbreak, he'd had no interest in joining in our little community. Frankie had always considered him an "uppity nigger." Frankie's errant bolt had caught Jordan in the calf, nothing serious, but it had riled things up like an anthill for a few days. Frankie responded just the way that I wanted, and it was an effort to keep my smile to myself. Getting him riled was fun.

"It was his own fault!" Frankie protested lightly, a false look of innocent humor on his face. "He shouldn't have been there in the first place! I was just trying to shoot a jack rabbit; I can't help it if he wandered in front of my shot."

I kept my smile to myself as Frankie continued his rant.

"Lewis can kiss my ass," he said, slinging the strap of the crossbow over his shoulder. "I'm bringin' Suzanna, but I'll bring Samantha, too, just to shut his pansy ass up."

Samantha was an old school katana sword, the type that you'd find at swap meets, carnivals, or mid-level smoke shops. The steel was rolled hard, with an acid washed edge that left a dull, serpentine line on one side. The sheath was wooden, painted mother of pearl white, and the hilt and straps were wrapped with purple nylon cord. It had a certain feminine quality that Frankie didn't want to hear shit about, and he'd spent hours- days, even- honing the edge until it was razor sharp. Not that it helped overly much.

Frankie was kind of a funny guy. Despite his hillbilly vernacular, he was highly intelligent. But he was still a hillbilly, and he loved his redneck good times. We'd gone out beyond the barrier together countless times, and he'd killed more than his fair share of deaders. But where I felt a release bordering on orgasm, Frankie tended to celebrate like a running back that had just won Super Bowl. In short, he viewed every kill like a hunter that had just brought down big game.

"Fuck *yeah*, donkey!" was his favorite line; I couldn't tell you why.

Frankie carried Samantha with him frequently when we went out. He'd brought down a lot of deaders with her, but it was always a sloppy affair; even more so than my bat. With my bat, at least, I knew exactly what I was doing, and could end it fast if I chose. When Frankie used Samantha … eh, that was a different story.

See, cutting off a head is much harder than you would think. It's not the deaders flesh that's the problem; that shit wilts like an apple three months out of season. It's the bones. Flesh may die, but bones stay as hard as they ever were. It's damn near impossible to cut through a neck unless you manage to hit the tiny space between the vertebrae. If you miss, the head just flops to the side from the impact and it keeps coming at you.

Not that that ever stopped Frankie. He would just hop back a bit and take another Babe Ruth swing. He had a tendency to hum "Welcome to the Jungle" by Guns 'N Roses when he did it. Once again, I couldn't tell you why. But I'd always liked that song, and when Frankie got at it, it always seemed to fit the mood.

We'd left the house that he and Lacy shared a few minutes ago, strolling down Branberry street. Frankie had the swagger of a high school quarterback going to Homecoming after having thrown the winning touchdown of the game. I walked the way that felt normal to me. I'd never recognized it as such, but it was a stride that the people of Branberry had learned meant I was out to do business.

We were only a dozen yards away from the wooden planked gate that was constructed across the mouth of the road when I heard a front door crack open from off to my right. Sure as shit, it was Nancy, belting out of her front door as Frankie and I strolled past. Her hair was undone from her typical tight bun, and her flaccid tits bounced as she jogged our direction.

"Are you going out?" she called, her voice tinged with desperation that I knew had nothing to do with our well being. I already knew where this was going.

"Nah, darlin'," Frankie called back with a smile, his pawn shop katana bobbing over his shoulder with every step. "We're just gonna walk up and down the street a few times; see if anything changes."

Nancy let the faintly veiled sarcasm roll over her and rushed up to us.

"See if you can find any Xanax," she said breathlessly. "Prozac, Zoloft; anything at all."

"I got some fresh 'shine back at the house," Frankie said with a mocking smile. "Take a few sips of that and you'll feel right as rain."

Nancy's face hardened into grim lines that made the wrinkles around her mouth stand out sharply. "I won't drink that swill; it's the Devil's work."

"You an' Sister Tracy been spendin' time together, again?" Frankie barbed as we walked past Nancy. "Hell, you go on an' tell'er I said hi. I'm goin' to find Jesus. Have you found Jesus, Nance? Want me to tell you where I find him?"

"Knock it off," I said under my breath, but there was no conviction behind it. I said it because it was the right thing to do, even though I secretly enjoyed hearing Frankie rip into my elderly neighbor. As expected, Frankie ignored me completely, and it didn't bother me in the least. My brother in law turned around, walking backwards, talking at the shrinking form of the perspiring woman standing in the middle of the street.

"I don't need you to find Jesus!" Nancy shrieked, her voice cracking. Her balled fists were shaking at her side like a three year old throwing a tantrum, "Find Chartreuse!"

Nancy stood there in silence with heated eyes, awaiting a response. Frankie and I had just reached the gate, but before we could climb over it he turned back to her. His face contorted in confusion, like she was speaking a foreign language.

"What *the fuck* is a Chartreuse?" he asked, spitting off to the side.

"It's her dog," I said under my breath, but still smiling to myself. Frankie was always good for a laugh. He played dumb, but he knew exactly what he was doing. Nancy wasn't quite as bright.

"Now, hell," he continued, his face a false mixture of confusion. "I thought those deaders killed your dog?"

Nancy looked ready to fly into a fury once more. Maybe the subject was that sensitive, or maybe she just needed her sedatives that badly. I wondered what she would do if she knew that Larry had packed a huge supply the day that Lewis and I had met him, and that I had it stored up in a spare bedroom of my house. She pointed a wild finger at me, and that little digit was chock full of accusation.

"You killed Verdance!" she shrieked, eyes full of righteous indignation. "Not the deaders!"

"Verdance?" Frankie asked, looking at me in a questioning manner. He was playing. I knew it and he knew it, but Nancy didn't. This was fun, so I played along with it.

"Her other dog. A deader ate him. Chartreuse ran off after I told her to go home."

It was true. After I'd taken down Pat, my high school sweetheart- admittedly killing Verdance in the process- the other Terrier had slipped out of its collar and run off. Nancy was still blaming me, though, rather than having an ounce of gratitude that I'd saved her life.

"Who names a dog that?" Frankie asked, face crinkling like someone- and a dirty someone, at that- had just defecated on his dinner. "Thor, Thunder; hell, even Bull or Shadow. T-Bone. Now, those are dog names. Char-*treusse?*" he asked, drawing the word out. "Damn, woman, that's like asking your dog to get raped by a cat. I ain't never known a good dog with a name like that."

Nancy looked ready to shriek again, but instead drew herself up to her full (less than intimidating) height. She huffed in offense, beads of sweat clinging to her hairline, and stormed back up to her house.

"Bye, Nance," Frankie called out jovially as the front door to the old bag's home slammed closed. "I'll let you know if I find Jesus!"

"Can we please get the fuck outta here, now?" Frankie continued, bending down and lacing his fingers together into a rough step for my foot.

"Yeah," I said as I put my very expensive sneaker into the web of his clasped hands. Frankie was a big guy, and it didn't take much for him to heave me up so that I could pull myself over the lip of the wall.

So what would you imagine lay beyond our gate? According to what pop culture told you, we should have been in the middle of the wilderness. Blank plains of grass that had run wild, stretching as far as the eye could see; Dense trees and shrubs. Maybe a dilapidated city that was scorched and blackened from fire run wild. We should have been terrified and ultra- alert the moment that our feet touched the ground. After all, hordes of deaders should have appeared immediately, wandering out of the woods, or rising from the fields of grass, or shambling from dark doorways …

You know what was over the wall? The other side of Branberry Street. I know; crazy, right? Try not to feel let down.

See, the entire enclosed block was laid out like a trident. The nearest major road was Mission Street, and it was just up the way. The route leading into our subdivision was Rocky Coast. From Rocky Coast, there were three cul de sacs, one of which was vacant, one of which others had moved into, and one of which was ours. Lewis and I might have been the first to erect a barrier, but the couple dozen people that took up residence on Rocky Coast had followed our lead pretty quick. The result was a wellfortified block with a bunch of relatively normal people going about what passed for normal lives.

As for the sudden appearance of deaders? Please, spare me. In the past however many months it had been we'd only had to repel three attacks, none of which had been overly concerning. Our walls were high, and- if I haven't made this clear, yet- deaders are none too bright. A pack of two or three dozen is easy to dismantle when they can't reach you. In addition to that, what I told Avery earlier in the day was true: if we stayed quiet, if we didn't give them a reason to notice us, they generally wandered on by without a second glance.

While wise, this often got boring to me. If I wanted a little bit of excitement, I had to go out to find it. Generally, that was in the large span of uncultivated desert that sat on the north side of our wall. We weren't *that* far from the epicenter of Las Vegas, and I could generally find one or two milling about.

"Hey, Martin!" Frankie called from beside me, waving to a lone figure that stood at the top of an A-frame ladder on the cul de sac next to ours. Middle aged Marvin waved back genially, hollering out.

"Hey, there, bud! You making a run?" Martin called. "What're you heading out for? We're looking pretty good over here. You need anything we might have?"

"Ain't that kind of run!" Frankie said with a yokel's stage chuckle, the kind that's generally reserved for high school boys going to a nudie bar for the first time. My potbellied brother in law held his arms wide- crossbow in one hand, and the sheathed Samantha in the other- and started to thrust his hips forward suggestively. The expression on his face was comical and absolutely vulgar at the same time.

Martin laughed. Frankie laughed. I pretended, and laughed, too. I think I did a pretty good job of pulling it off. I may not have understood the joke, but Martin and his block were part of our group, even if just by proxy. I wanted to be polite; it was always good to be polite.

"Should have known," Martin called back, gesturing to me. "Exterminator's don't go out without a reason."

"Cletus, here?" Frankie drawled. "Hell, I wouldn't be caught dead out here without ol' Cleet by my side."

"Anything in particular that we should keep an eye out for?" I called up to Martin. I was only halfway trying to be part of the conversation. Don't get me wrong; we all needed something, plenty of things, but it was the little stuff that we'd all learned mattered the most. Remember, duct tape, zip ties, and super glue could make your world a happier place. "Shoe laces!" Martin called after a moment of consideration. The request surprised me, but only for a second. After all, in Deaderland, no request should have been a shock. Frankie wasn't so subtle.

"What the hell do ya need shoelaces for?" he called as we continued to walk past.

"For shoes, you idiot!" Martin replied, his face breaking into a wide grin. "Nah, we use 'em for bindings. We're building an awning; Gonna have a wedding this afternoon. You and your crew should join us."

"You should try zip ties," my brother in law said, but Martin shook his head. "Nah, we don't have anymore, and we don't want to waste any rope or bungees."

"Shit, zip ties are what me an' Cleet are going out for," Frankie said. "If we can find any we'll bring you back a few extra. Give our regards to the newlyweds, will ya?"

"Will do," Martin replied. "Frank," he said with a goodbye wave before giving me a salute and a humorous smirk. "Cleet."

Great, I thought. *Another person calling me Cletus.*

"Bahmp ... bahmp ... bahmp," Frankie said next to me, singing under his breath as we walked up Mission street. *"Another one bites the dust ... Bahmp ... bahmp..bah-"*

"Will you shut the fuck up?" I said, turning my head to regard him. Frankie stopped, and didn't look offended in the least. He seemed to have a higher tolerance for my moods than some of the others on Branberry. Maybe that was one of the reasons we got along so well.

"What's got your panties in a bunch, sweetness?" he asked. I shrugged it off.

"I just don't like that song."

"Shit," Frankie said, mollified. "Why didn't you just say so?"

"I did; just now."

Mission street was a fairly steep road, and in the fifteen minutes or so that we'd been walking we'd probably only covered about a mile. The road- like so many of them were- was empty. Most people that weren't Exterminators didn't venture too far away from safety if they didn't have to. There were plenty of stores and shops in the outlying area, but in this section on the outskirts of Vegas, most of the undeveloped area was desert. Not "desert" like films you've seen showing off the Sahara; city desert. It was rocky and bumpy, covered with sagebrush and the sparse branches of desert trees. Garbage and refuse- old tires, beer cans, the occasional washer from circa 1962- littered the ground in abundance.

Most people don't realize that deserts have trees, but they do. The branches are bare, sun bleached, and are often sharp and brittle. We'd thought about burning it down in the first few weeks. After all, twenty or thirty acres of dense shrubbery wasn't conducive to a clear line of sight. In the end, we'd left it standing because we trusted our walls and defenses, and we didn't want to destroy anything that we might have been able to use later on. It had been Lew's suggestion, and I'd been fine with it. Those bushes held a few more deaders than he realized, and I slipped out every now and again to finish a few off. It helped keep my needs at bay. But we did clear out a nice, neat section around the perimeter of our wall.

"Hey, Cleet," Frankie said, breaking my fond reverie from four and a half days ago. "You feel up to a bit of a ruckus?"

"Ruckus?"

"Yeah. Get a bit batshit; a little bit of trouble. You know; red neck good times."

Frankie pointed the sheathed tip of Samantha's scabbard off over my shoulder, like the Great Bambino pointing out a home run. I turned to look, even though I had a pretty good idea what he was pointing at: the I-95 highway.

Cinema got it right when it came to highways. When the pandemic started to really take effect, a lot of people did flee. Traffic on the highway had been bumper to bumper not so much because of the exodus, but because the fools had done it during rush hour. People died, and I'll leave it to your imagination to figure out how. Most of the bodies were gone, but the dead dinosaurs that were their vehicles remained.

Highways were a double edged sword for any of us that wanted to travel along them. You couldn't drive a car up them because of the congestion. The maze of dead vehicles also made it impossible for bicycles. If you had a long way to walk, however, the highway was generally the fastest way to go. Not that many people walked that far from home, but if they did … well, the shortest distance between two points is a straight line.

There was a lot to scavenge if you were so inclined to dig through the muck and dried blood, but the downside was that highways were prone to a lot of deader movement. If you found yourself in a sticky situation, you only had three ways to go: forward or back, through an obstacle course of cars and refuse, or over the concrete barrier, which was a twenty foot fall. None of these were good options, and even I rarely ventured into that jungle of iron and fiberglass.

"We ain't gotta go far," Frankie implored, but he didn't have to convince me. Although I only used the 95 when I had to, my need was pulling at me and making my skin itch. Frankie's notion seemed like a fantastic idea. The walk would only take about another fifteen minutes. We could go out, have some red neck good times, and then head back down to more familiar areas to do our supply scrounging. In the end, it wasn't much of a decision at all. We'd get our scavenging done as promised, but we both knew that had been just a pretense to get out. We'd gone over the wall with one purpose.

The walk was a short one. We cut through the arid desert, half hoping to have a little fun before we got to the 95. Each of us carried a handgun -it was an unspoken law that you had to be armed. I had my Sig, and Frankie carried a Glock .45- but they stayed holstered at our hips. Suzannah was slung across his back (the crossbow would be almost useless in the dense brush) but he carried Samantha naked in his hand as we pushed our way through. We walked unhurriedly through the desert, but had seen nothing by the time we reached the freeway onramp. Too bad.

The crowded entrance to the 95 was littered with refuse, but nothing readily usable. Most of the good stuff had been taken from the first few rows of vehicles long before people realized that it was wiser to stay away from the freeway. Our feet crunched on the broken asphalt as we moved up the steep, curving incline.

"Ah," Frankie said from my left. "That's what we need."

He reached down and picked up a rusty tire iron that was lying near the cement wall. It wasn't one of the T bars that had four heads; it was a stock "L," the type that came in the survival kits that most cars had tucked beneath the rear seat or side compartment.

"D'wayne has plenty of those at home," I said.

"Nah, I ain't lookin' to take it home," Frankie said, giving it a whirl in his hand. He twirled about with a grace that was odd in a man his size, and smashed out the window of a sun faded red car. It was older; the type of nameless older model that I had generally started to dub "a 1987 Daihatsu Surprise." The glass exploded in a tinkling crash that sounded loud in the silence of the freeway. Frankie hooted to himself, giving the tire iron another twirl.

"I have a bat," I said dryly. "You could have just told me."

"Ain't no fun in that!" he said, grinning his yellowed grin. "Why tell you when I can do it myself? Besides, this is a healthy show of aggression; helps to relieve the tensio- huh?"

Frankie cut off in mid-sentence, his enthusiasm evaporating as his eyes focused on the interior of the vehicle. He ducked his head, squinting, and I wondered if maybe there was a deader cat in the back seat. Wouldn't have been the first time that we'd found one. The virus could spread to a few different breeds of animal, and cats in particular were mean little fuckers. I realized that I shouldn't have gotten my hopes up when Frankie's eyes widened with glee, and he let out a whooping yell like a child on Christmas morning.

"Look at this, Cleet!" he shouted, reaching an arm in through the broken window to pop the door of the Surprise open from the inside. His front half disappeared, and all I saw were his ass and feet as he dug through something that I couldn't see. He seemed happy enough, so I didn't have any cause for worry.

"Aw, shit," he exclaimed- he drew the word out until it sounded like *shee-yit-* his excitement rising to a new level. "By the baby Jesus, I love hillbillies."

"Whaddya got?" I called over, my curiosity piqued. Frankie clambered out of the back seat with a wide, shit eating grin on his face.

"Somethin' for both of us," he said proudly, and if anything his smile got wider. He held out a crumpled red hat, the front and bill tinged with layers of old sweat stains. On the front was a circular profile of an Indian, the logo for Florida State University. "Hail, 'Noles!" he yelled, popping the filthy cap onto his head. Frankie didn't have much hair; he kept everything close to the scalp, maintaining it on a semi daily basis. I, on the other hand, hadn't bothered to cut my hair in months, and it dangled at my shoulders, longer than it had ever been.

"That's disgusting," I said, wondering if some of the darker splotches might not be blood stains from the previous owner. When a deader managed to sink its teeth into you there generally wasn't anything left but gnawed bone and the bits and pieces that it couldn't reach. It was a messy affair.

"It's pride is what it is, you pussy," Frankie jested lightly, giving the bill of the cap a firm yank, "You don't ever let your team down, and they won't ever let you down." He smiled like he'd imparted some universal enlightenment. That was Frankie; the Sun Tzu of North Dakota.

"Here's the coup de grace, though," he continued, holding out his other hand. Frankie's meaty palm was wrapped around the neck of a white labeled bottle filled with brown liquid. My mouth immediately began to water.

"Is that-?" I began.

"Yep! Kentucky's Finest, brewed from the recipe of Mister Beam, hisself!"

Frankie's moonshine was alcohol if we wanted it, but it could also strip paint or degrease an engine. Of all the things that we'd prioritized in the early days, refined alcohol hadn't been one of them. The bottle was sealed, but my brother in law cracked it open with a quick twist of his hand, throwing it back to take a long swig. He wiped his chin and held the bottle out to me. I remembered how Avery had backwashed into the water bottle earlier in the day, and I can't say that Frankie was much better. But this was Jim Beam, and alcohol killed germs. Right?

I took the bottle eagerly enough, taking a long pull from the side that Frankie's lips hadn't touched. It had been a good long while since I'd had commercial liquor, and it burned my mouth as I swallowed. I'd just pulled the rim from my lips when I heard a loud, whooping bark from somewhere ahead of us. I knew that sound; we both did.

Deaders don't roar; they don't shriek. What they have is a loud, whoomping cough, much like lions did on the old Discovery Channel documentaries. It was deep, it reverberated, and it was a sign to the rest of their pack that they had found prey. It was also how the kept in contact with each other.

"Fuck yeah!" Frankie yelled, his face lighting up with enthusiasm. He cocked his new/used Seminoles cap up his forehead, and pulled Suzannah from his back. He knocked one of the half dozen bolts he'd brought with him, grunting as his fingers strained to pull the shortened drawstring back. I set the bottle of Beam on the trunk of the Daihatsu Surprise, and Frankie tossed me the cap to screw back on. No point in wasting anything that served a purpose, after all.

If we didn't seem rushed it was only because we knew that we had a few minutes to spare. What we were both waiting on was a call from its peers so that we knew how many we were dealing with. I counted to myself, much like waiting for the clap of thunder that follows a lightning strike. I could see Frankie's lips moving soundlessly as he did the same.

One … two … three … four …

"*Broomp!*" a hacking, coughing call echoed out. It was deep; a male, then. One more confirmed, then. Frankie was looking more eager by the second, and his body was beginning to jive back and forth to the unsung rhythm of what I knew to be "Welcome to the Jungle."

One, two, thre-

"*Broomp!*" … "*Broomf!*"

Two more; one male, one female. We waited, Frankie becoming more eager by the second as I sunk down into the dark place where my needs lived. It was time to focus; my release was coming. Some distant part of me took note that Frankie had started humming. That was always a portent of good things to come. Seconds ticked by, but there were no more calls. Four, then.

"Let's get these donkeys," Frankie said. "Gimme a shot first before you close on'em; I wanna see how Suzannah is working, now."

It was an odd request, but Frankie was an odd guy. He'd been hunting turkey in the forests of Hicktown before most people are out of Pampers, and that skill had followed him into the enlisted ranks of the United States Military as a field sniper. I don't know how good he'd been at his job, but the fact that he'd found his way home spoke volumes. I'd never bothered to ask him how many people he'd killed, the same way that he'd never bothered to ask me. We were just a couple of whores that had an unspoken understanding.

My brother in law was an amazing shot with his crossbow, but it was a tricky thing with deaders. Beating their heads to a pulp had its own dangers, but it was easy. To kill them with an arrow? That took a different type of finesse. You had to go straight through the eye, at just the right angle. As I mentioned earlier, the cranium is one of the hardest parts of the body, and-when hitting them in the forehead- the bolt just didn't have enough power to drive deeply enough into the gray matter to hit the off switch. Essentially, unless you got lucky, the realistic expectation that you could hope for with an arrow was to take out an eye on things that were probably half blind to begin with. Hit a leg or shoulder? Remember, they don't respond to pain the way that you and I do. But we were out for a ruckus, right?

"Yeah, Frank," I said, my voice cold but breathless with eagerness. I was in my dark place, my cold place; the type of place that Charles Darwin would have felt comfortable. After all, if this wasn't survival of the fittest, I didn't know what was. "Take your shot."

Frankie reached into one of his pockets and pulled out an aged can of Grizzly chewing tobacco. That can had gone dry a long time ago, but he had continued to fill it with his own shredded leaves. Like I said; recycle. He tucked a pinch into his lip, and then set the stock of the crossbow against his shoulder. At the last moment, I remembered to pull the bandana tied around my neck up over my face to cover my nose and mouth.

"Get at it, then," he said in a flat voice, and I flowed forward like a ghost that had just been invited into a home. I worked my way between the weaving press of vehicles, keeping my back close to the metal doors and hoods. Frankie trailed behind me like a shadow, the steel tip of his bolt moving back and forth with his line of sight. We stalked this way- me taking the lead with Frankie as my back up- for a hundred yards before we found the lead deader.

He was a big son of a bitch, towering over me by close to a foot. Like all deaders, his flesh and skin had shriveled away, wrapping his skull like rotten shrink wrap. The hair had fallen from his head, half his teeth were missing, and the desiccated form was wearing the tattered remains of a UCLA pull over hoodie. If the sweatshirt was to be believed, this one had covered some distance, and was still mostly intact despite it. I started to run towards it when I heard Frankie call out from behind me.

"Shot!" I hollered, reminding me that I'd promised to give him the first go. I dropped down on my haunches, the deader maybe a dozen steps in front of me. It's clouded eyes had just started to notice me as I heard the sharp *twang* of Frankie pulling the trigger to the crossbow. A wispy hiss cut the air over my head, and the bolt took the deader on the left side of its nose, ripping through the dehydrated flesh. The arrow barely slowed as it barreled through the back of the skull and soared out over the freeway's edge. The deader's head snapped back from the impact, and if it hadn't been for the support of the SUV behind it, it would have fallen. As it was, it pulled itself upright with nary a flinch or shake of its head.

"*Ho-lee shee-yit!*" Frankie yelled, jubilant. "Did you see that?"

Yes, Frankie; I saw that. I was here when it happened. But it's still alive, and now it's my turn.

I barreled forward, leaping onto the hood of a car. In the distant background, I heard Frankie shouting out the opening line of "Welcome to the Jungle."

The deader turned its milky eyes at me. It tried to snarl, to howl, but the lower side of its jaw was gone where Frankie's bolt had ripped it clean off. The result was a disgusting gurgling that caused the ruined face to gyrate. Creamy white orbs laced with bloody cataracts turned black pupils my way, uncaring that the lower half of its face was gone.

Standing on the hood of the car as I was, the head of the towering deader was a couple feet below me. Its eyes trailed up my way as it lashed out with a gnarled fingered hand. *Stupid bastard,* I thought with a gleeful, internal chuckle, *you're too slow.* The end of my bat cracked into its temple with a hollow, *ting* sound. Stagnant black blood splashed out of the head as the side of the skull caved in. The corpse fell, never giving any indication that it had felt an ounce of pain … or remorse … or semblance of the person he used to be.

UCLA hit the ground with a thud. There was a good sized concavity in the side of his head, and from between the shards of skull I could see maggots wiggling. Their pale, worm-like bodies wriggled back and forth, some searching for deep cover while others were brave enough to squiggle their way out of the broken calcium coffin.

I had to kill them. I smashed my bat down a few more times, and then stomped any of the pests that made their way free- inching their way across the highway- beneath the heel of my shoe. You had to be careful with maggots. They weren't dangerous- in the sense that they would attack you- but they carried the infection. They gave it to the birds that ate them. The birds gave it to the cats that killed them. The cats gave it to …

You get the point. This, we think, is part of the reason that the infection spread as fast as it did. As an example: Cattle went rabid in Texas and Montana, gone feral from the grass that they ate, grass that was contaminated by their own shit stuck in the curves of their hooves, shit that was contaminated by the worms in their stool … The animals were put down in what I'm sure was a very humane fashion, sliced up into neat little steaks, and then shipped off to market.

Moral of the story? Kill maggots when you see them. Trust me; it makes sense.

"Good kill!" Frankie yelled enthusiastically as he trotted up my way, his work boots trampling a few of the squirming maggots that had escaped my attention. "Did you see that shit?" he repeated, "I didn't think cutting the cord down would make it that strong."

"Well, it worked," I panted with the exertion of adrenaline as I wiped my bat off on the limp deader's hoodie. "Focus up, though; we've got three more."

"Right," Frankie said, spitting a thick brown stream off to the side through pursed lips as he fit another bolt into his crossbow. "You wanna take lead, or you want me to get in there?"

"I got lead," I said. To be honest, I never liked sharing the lead position. I trusted Frankie; I trusted his accuracy … but I didn't like giving up any of my kills. UCLA had been the tip of the iceberg, but now I was ready to get some real work in. "Hey," I said, breathless with enthusiasm, "sing that song again."

"Which one?"

"*Bahmp, bahmp, bahmp,*" I sang, imitating his deeper voice as best as I could, "*another one bites the dust.*"

Pause. "Thought you said you didn't like it?"

"It fits."

"A'right, then."

We moved forward on full alert, Frankie singing under his breath. We knew that the other three deaders had to be close. As much as they seemed to work on their own agenda, when they found each other they had a tendency to stay relatively close together. This is how the packs formed, and it might have been the last vestige of humanity that they had left. The others couldn't have been far, so we worked our way up the highway, moving about the clusters of vehicles with the type of practiced precision that came with the comfort of dozens of hunts together. We were rewarded after a hundred yards or so.

"Broomp!"

"Broomp! ... Broomp!"

I'd barely had a moment to tense up before I heard the creaking thump of metal bending. The lead deader- another male- had leapt onto the hood of another car just off to my left. Its right arm was gone, ripped away at the elbow. The nub was hidden by the tattered sleeves of his shirt, but there was no disguising the wide shoulders and narrow waist of an experienced athlete. It sat there, propped up on three appendages like an image from a comic book, gazing around with the dead intensity that I'd come to expect. The other two weren't far behind.

One was a middle aged male, dressed in the tattered remains of a white dress shirt and black tie. While it had deflated as the corpse had aged, there was more than a bit of beer belly on him. The second- female- stood close to his hand. Judging by the ragged strands of shoulder length blonde hair hanging from her scalp and the ample amount of decaying bosom, she might have been pretty before she had been infected.

I didn't spare them too much consideration; it was time to kill.

I moved forward around the bumper of a car, swinging my bat at the lead male- the athlete's- ankle. A tip from the pros? Always, *always,* attack first if you can. It's always better to be acting than *reacting.* The creature surprised us both, though. Rather than attack me- the closest- he darted off to the side, slipping out of the reach of my bat and bounding across the hoods of nearby cars with an eerie, arachnid ease. I heard the twang of Frankie's crossbow, but since the deader had changed direction so suddenly the bolt flew over the edge of the freeway. Slick as he was, Frankie didn't have time to reload.

The deader landed within a few feet of him, coughing and hacking, noxious green spittle dangling from shriveled lips. Frankie cursed, his song cutting off in mid chorus. Susannah dropped from his hands to dangle on his back strap. His hand dipped towards his holstered .45 out of instinct, but then stopped and moved towards Samantha's haft. He pulled the katana from its sheathe faster and more gracefully than you'd imagine a man his size was capable of just as the deader took a swipe at his face with its remaining arm.

Honestly, my brother in law should have died a slow death, right then and there. Frankie had a killer's trained reflexes, but the deader was faster than he was. It was sheer, blind luck that saved him. The athlete's swipe connected with the side view mirror of the vehicle, giving just enough time for Frankie to leap back.

"Fuck, donkey!" he spat as he hacked Samantha into its hand like a lumberjack. Three shriveled digits fell to the asphalt at his feet, but the athletic deader didn't hesitate in the slightest, continuing to clamber forward. Beer Belly and Used to be Pretty picked up their pace and followed him, centering on the heavyset, ex-soldier hillbilly with the FSU cap perched on his brow.

There were still two cars separating us, and I weaved around them as Frankie swung a second time. The hardened blade glanced off of the athlete's skull, but took a thick flap of brown skin with it. I had managed to get close enough, and the deader's ass was propped up in the air as I cracked my bat into its extended leg, right at the knee. The tip of the silver Louisville connected with a crunch, and the deader flopped to the side as it lost its precarious balance.

The deader continued to cough and hack, reaching its maimed hand Frankie's direction. Lying flat on the hood of the car- with a shattered knee, no less- it didn't make much progress. Frankie stepped forward with a savage grin and chopped his pawn shop katana down onto the hairless skull. The rolled steel blade wasn't particularly heavy, but the edge could split a hair and Frankie was a strong guy. The sword split the cranium, driving deep into the dehydrated brain with the sound of a sledgehammer smashing a melon. The creature groaned, twitched, and then went limp. We didn't have time to celebrate, though; the other two had drawn within arms reach.

Frankie gave the hilt of the sword a tug, but the blade was stuck fast. He gave up on it and pulled up the crossbow dangling near his hip. His hands worked to place another bolt, but the stubborn drawstring was too hard to pull with one hand. The arrow tumbled loose, and fell over the edge of the freeway. For the moment, Frankie was defenseless, and that meant it was my turn.

I dashed forward, jumping and sliding over the hood of a car like it was the General Lee and I was Bo Duke. Beer Belly was within reach, and I cracked my bat across his pelvis as I slid. There was a loud *ting* of impact as the aluminum connected with the hard bone of its hip, but the strike didn't have enough power behind it to do any real damage. I'm sure it looked *really* cool, though.

I landed on my feet as I slid off the other side of the hood and rose, still swinging. I cracked Beer Belly across the wrist to knock its reaching hand aside, and then struck the inside of its lead knee as hard as I could. The joint crunched, buckled, and the deader stumbled just long enough for me to bust it across the temple. It toppled silently to the side like a garbage bag filled with meat and bone.

I whirled on the remaining female, but Used to be Pretty had stopped, not attacking the way that I would have expected her to. A soft, thin mewl whispered between her lips as she looked at Beer Belly's lifeless, oozing form, and then she turned her milky eyes on me. I didn't know I had the ability for this type of fear driven reaction, but I stopped in my tracks. A deader's gaze is a vacant thing, much like a running car in neutral pushed down a high hill; the engine might be running, but there's no one behind the wheel, so to speak. I couldn't tell you what it was, but Used to be Pretty was different. There was an alertness in her eyes, an odd awareness that was somehow-

No; can't be.

-thinking.

Used to be Pretty took a measured, calculated step out of my reach, and there was no denying the undisguised hatred for me on her mottled, shrunken face. Her still generous cleavage expanded as she drew in a deep breath before giving a loud "*Brooooooomf!*" that I could feel reverberating through my eardrums. The resounding call had just died out when I watched the feathered shaft of one of Frankie's arrows plant itself in the center of her forehead. The quarrel exploded through the rear of her skull and sailed out over the edge of the freeway, much as the other had done.

The female deader crumbled, flopping over backwards. She landed in a heap with her skirt flipped up over her waist to expose her girly parts, and her flower print panties were dark and soiled with filth. The echoes of her call were still ringing in the air.

"Holy fuck stick, Cleet," Frankie gasped, calm despite the confrontation and close brush with infection. It wasn't surprising; we'd both done this enough times that a good, solid adrenaline rush wasn't the same thing as fear. "That first fucker almost took my face off."

"Probably would've been doing you a favor," I said, panting slightly as I nudged UCLA with my toe. You could never be too careful with these things. The body shifted rigidly, and gradually slid off the car hood to collapse in a lump. My nose crinkled; God, these things smelled bad. "You need to lose some weight, anyway. Gotta start somewhere."

Frankie gave a couple hefty slaps to his paunch. "I'm all man, pussy," he said lightly, with a jovial smile. "Where'd we leave that Beam at?" he continued, refocusing on priorities. "I could use a swig. Mr. Beam knew how to do it right."

"Back down the way," I replied absently as I walked over to look at the ruined features of Used to be Pretty. Now that she'd been put down she looked no different than any other deader. But she'd been aware, somehow, in a way that I hadn't seen before. It was disturbing, and there was very little in the world that disturbed me. Now she was just another lifeless meat sack, and I couldn't glean any answers from the shattered remains of her face. With a last considering glance, I turned to follow Frankie back down the highway.

I reveled silently in the wonderful sense of relief I felt as I caught up with my brother in law. I gave him a nod, and he wordlessly held the knuckles of his closed fist out my way. I bumped my own knuckles against them, and we continued back down the onramp of the I-95. We'd gone maybe fifteen yards in silence when a chorus of distant calls erupted. It sounded like a massive pack of hyenas, but to the best of my knowledge, there were no hyenas in Vegas.

We both stopped, our eyes turning to the west. With almost a year of no traffic, the ever present haze that hung about the Las Vegas Strip had dissipated. The hotels and casinos were as tall and massive as ever, and from this distance you couldn't even see how dilapidated they had become. Some might have thought it was a pretty sight, but I'd been seeing it for so many years that I didn't notice it. What we *were* focused on was the sound of those cries, and what it meant. It was a pack, and judging by the number of whooping, barking coughs, a big one. It was the type that I would advise my own people to run- as fast as you could- away from.

Frankie and I shared a look just as another set of calls took up from slightly further north. They were even more muted than the first group, but it wasn't hard to deduce that they were only a handful of miles apart. Eager as we both were for some redneck good times, we both knew that a pack that size- let alone two- was well beyond our skill set.

Yep," Frankie said in a philosophical way, his eyes turned off towards the horizon, "now I definitely need another drink."

We didn't necessarily *hurry* back down the onramp, but we didn't move at the leisurely pace we'd started out with, either. The packs- both packs- were miles away, and had no reason to even know of our existence. They'd undoubtedly picked up the call of the female deader that Frankie had put down, but beyond a vague direction they couldn't possibly know where we were. Still, that was no reason to abandon common sense. We only made one brief stop, and that was at the Surprise so that each of us could take another deep swig from the bottle.

"Bring it?" Frankie suggested, holding the still plenty full bottle up. I gave it a moment of consideration.

"Nah," I replied. I was already starting to feel a bit light headed. "Tuck it in the trunk. I don't really want to share it, and this way we know where it is the next time we come out."

Frankie thought about it, then nodded in agreement. Mr. Beam's recipe was too good to partition out, after all. We emerged from the 95 onramp no worse the wear despite our "ruckus," and turned south to where our rummaging grounds are. We'd had our fun, but now it was time for us to get to the work/ excuse that we'd come out here for. Although it was miles away, we could still hear the sporadic yips and yelps of the two packs of deaders.

"You wanna get your arrows?" I asked as we rounded the last bend of the freeway. I'd noticed that he was down to his last one.

"Nah," he said, brushing it off with a wave of his hand. "I got plenty back home. I didn't expect Susannah to have that much power. I wouldn't even know where to look for the bolts that flew off, anyway."

Sounded good to me. I didn't want to waste my approved day out on a pointless search around the desert for the needle in the proverbial haystack. We rounded the curve of the road, heading down to the dilapidated area where we did most of our "shopping." It was a funny little area of Vegas that we called home. On one side of the freeway you had the "well to do" neighborhoods. Three miles the other direction, however, you found yourself in hillbilly Hender-tucky, capital of Podunk Town. Honestly? If those hillbilly meth- heads had banded together, they probably would have flourished. Maybe even better than we ourselves had. Call'em what you will, but red necks were survivors, and they had an odd and surprising list of skills and abilities.

As it was, though, most of them got too aggressive in the beginning, seeing the zombie apocalypse as just another excuse to drink beer, smoke dope, blow shit up, and promote the general idea of anarchy. They were just as effective at wiping themselves out as the deaders were, and had left us as the survivors with a veritable treasure trove of random shit that stretched out over dozens of square miles of hillbilly heaven. There were trailer parks, dumpsters, and even a few landfills. These were all interspersed with the beautiful neighborhoods that had been filled with rich people that hadn't had the foresight- and common sense- that those of us on Branberry had. If for whatever reason we ever ran out of room in our little compound, we knew where we could find a nice double wide to drag in.

Frankie and I spent a couple of hours searching through the sprawling mesh of trailers and mobiles, trying to focus on ones that we hadn't really been into, yet. I don't want you to think we were working too hard, though. Honestly, it was a great time for both of us. We smashed shit, broke windows, rummaged around, gathered things that we found useful as well as the items on the list that we'd brought with us. Frankie shoveled everything into his green duffle. There was no discrimination in our world; all of our supplies could live happily together, no matter what purpose they served.

We ran into four more deaders over the course of our exploration, each one wandering by themselves. See, the funny thing about deaders? If they don't find a pack- if they don't have any of their own around them- they tend to stay in the same little areas that they used to inhabit. They don't really feel the need to move unless they hear the call of a pack or something they can kill walks into their vicinity. Frankie and I took them down easily- one by one- and had a blast as we did so. One of them, a skinny, narrow shouldered male in a stained wife beater tank top even had a treasure hanging across his chest in the form of a heavily stocked bandolier.

"Ah, hell yeah," Frankie crowed in excitement as he knelt down next to the deader that had just stopped kicking. "These're thirty aught sixes."

"I don't know what that means," I said flatly from where I stood, keeping an eye out for any others.

"Rifle shells, Cletus!" he chortled, pulling the bandolier off of the scrawny deader and stuffing it into his duffle. The belt would probably have to go- it was undoubtedly contaminated- but the shells were still good. "These'll fit my Springfield!"

"Amazing."

"You're Goddamn right, it's amazing," Frankie crowed, flashing the grin that told me he was fully enveloped in his red neck good times. "Now, let's see what else we got," he said, delving into the pockets of the deaders black jeans. I could see his hidden fingers rustling beneath the fabric over the skinny hips.

"Ah, what do we got, here?" he sighed, pulling his hand out. His fingers were clasping a small plastic baggie filled with white powder. Frankie shook it back and forth.

"Looks like coke," I said, my lips shriveling in disdain.

"Nah, country boys like this can't afford coke," Frankie countered. "This here's heroine."

"I don't care if it's fucking ambrosia," I said. "Toss it; I don't want that shit anywhere near Branberry."

"Stop being such a puss, sweetness," Frankie said without any heat. He held the baggie up to me. "This here is an opiate, just like morphine. Percocet, Percodan, Oxycodone … it's all the same shit. It kills pain. Hell, they used to use this like candy back in World War II. It won't hurt us to hold on to it; throw it in Larry's stockpile, just in case."

Frankie's face split into a devilish grin as an idea hit him, and he rummaged about in his duffle for a moment before emerging with a pack of Sharpie markers that we'd found earlier. He pulled one out, popping the cap off with his thumb, and started to write on the clear plastic baggie.

"*Jee-sus,*" he sounded out at he wrote, smiling to himself. He held the baggie out to me once more for inspection. "I should give this to Nancy!" he exclaimed proudly. "Tell'er I found Jesus! That'll shut'er up for a minute!"

"Nancy is one of ours," I said. Something in my face or tone must have changed, because the smile dropped from Frankie's expression.

"What was it you said earlier?" I asked, "take care of your team and they'll take care of you?"

Frankie's shoulders slumped and his face flushed, a bit. "Shit, you don't have to be a whiny bitch about it."

That was as close as I could expect to Frankie telling me I was right.

"Put it in the bag," I sighed. That was as close as Frankie would get from me. We understood each other, and my brother in law tossed it into the duffle. "What time is it?" he asked.

I glanced at the solar powered watch on my wrist. It wasn't anything nearly as fancy as a Rolex or Bulgari; quite the contrary. It was a kids velcro watch, and had a small gray bar along the face that allowed the sun to fuel it. I couldn't have told you how accurate it was, but it gave us some idea of the time, and was a damn sight better than trying to watch the sun trail across the sky. "Quarter to four," I said.

"We got most everything we need?"

I ran through my mental list. We'd managed to find almost everything we'd been scrounging for, including Martin's shoelaces and Lacy's zipties. Although I'd never allow her to even see it, I could even count the baggie of heroin towards Nancy's Zoloft. I nodded to Frankie.

"Probably about time to be heading back, yeah? Lacy pitches a fit if I'm gone too long."

I sighed, but didn't argue. I may not have been married to her, but I knew my sister. "Yeah. Figure we'll get back there, what, around four thirty?"

"'bout three miles, or so," Frankie said, turning the numbers over in his head. "Yeah, sounds about right."

"Wanna race?" I asked with a smile as Frankie shouldered his duffle. He gave me a look like I was stupid.

"Do I look like I run anywhere?" he quipped back, gesturing to himself. Frankie was broad in the shoulders but equally broad in the belly, and the combination of Samantha, Suzannah, and his duffle was understandably cumbersome. I snorted in humor, but cut off as my eyes caught a flash of color fluttering near the wheel of one of the mobile homes.

I walked over and plucked it up from beneath the tire. It was a small, ragged square of white wax paper with a jubilant yellow smiley face sticker in the center of it. Roughly the size of a baseball, the sticker was the type that a grocery store clerk used to give small children for good behavior while they waited in the checkout line. I fancied it, and peeled the decal off, letting the wax paper flutter away in the breeze. I pressed it onto the face of my bat and regarded it. The sticker gave me a jovial, frozen grin, and I smiled back.

"That's some gay ass shit, right there," Frankie said. I turned my upright bat to face him, so that he could get a good look at the lifeless black eyes and frozen smile.

"Don't worry; be happy," I said, starting to whistle a tune I'd heard in my youth as I turned to begin the walk back to Branberry. The song wasn't as good as "Welcome to the Jungle," but it was close.

Man's Best Friend

Things went ass up when we were about a mile from home.

Remember the packs we'd heard while on the freeway? The yipping, coughing yells like hyenas in the distance? The packs that couldn't *possibly* have any idea where we were beyond a vague direction? Well, they'd gotten closer. A lot closer.

"Drones," Frankie whispered, tilting his face over my shoulder to peek around the edge of a brick wall. We were both tucked tight against the wall of what used to be a grocery superstore, doing our best to stay in the shadows and keep out of any direct line of sight. Frankie had a huge plug of tobacco tucked in his lip as we surveyed the layout. He wasn't spitting, though; we couldn't risk the sound.

In case you've never seen one, drones are the equivalent of an army scout. They venture out from the pack, but never get so far away that the rest of the group can't hear them when they call. A small pack might have one or two; a larger as many as eight to ten. It's hard to explain how to know the difference between a drone and your average deader. They moved differently, more along the lines of Romero's depiction of zombies. They were (slightly) less aggressive, and somehow even more mindless. But they would bark at anything that caught their attention; this could be anything from prey to a random beam of light reflecting off of a piece of broken glass.

A handful of them wasn't an issue, if you knew what you were doing. Actually, it could be fun; like shooting fish in a barrel. Circle around behind them, sneak up, couple sharp cracks of the bat- *ting, ting-* and they'd never even get a call off. But this … this was different. There were dozens- scores, even- of drones wandering across the cross street that we'd been heading up; the street that was heading to home. Worse than that, they were moving in mixed pairs, much as Beer Belly and Used to be Pretty had been.

Frankie and I were both good at what we did. Hell, we both *loved* what we did. Put him and me together in the desert with a dozen deaders to take down, and that was *my* version of redneck good times. But our current situation was different. This was where I would take my own advice and run; just go the other way. Problem was, there were too many of them fanned out across the parking lot and street that we needed to cross for us to do any such thing. All roads may lead home, but the road that most certainly *did* lead home was covered in deaders.

I was gazing down the open road of Mission street, the road that lead down to the entrance at Branberry. It was maybe a half mile off, but there were at least three dozen deaders spread and paired off in the distance. The run down Mission to Rocky Coast was another quarter mile. They might be mindless and halfway retarded, but drones are just as quick as any other deader when something catches their attention.

"Might be about time for the ammo, Cleet," Frankie said, breathing deeply. His tobacco scented breath was heavy against my cheek as he gazed over my shoulder around the building. His hand started to dip to the handle of his .45.

"Not yet," I whispered, resisting my own urge to pull my Sig out. "Give it a minute; let this group get past us. We can use the space behind them to make our run."

"What if there isn't a space?" he countered stubbornly, echoing my own turbulent thoughts. "What's the plan, then?"

I didn't have an answer, but was saved from being forced to admit it as a loud noise erupted from the other side of the grocery store that we were taking cover against. A clatter of metal, a loud "*Broomf!*" and a strangled yelp. A rat, a cat, a scavenging coyote … I couldn't have cared less. All of the drones halted, their heads turning as one at the ruckus. I felt Frankie tense up behind me.

"Wait," I implored in a hushed tone, putting my hand against his thigh. "Give it a second."

In a shambling line that was quickly picking up speed, dozens of deaders started to move towards the opposite side of the grocery store like a colony of ants milling from their hill. I felt a strong urge to throw myself against them, but common sense won out. When all of their attention was directed at the other side of the building I slapped Frankie on the leg. "Now."

Frankie and I bolted, running bent over at the waist, ducking and hiding behind deserted vehicles in the parking lot. We'd wait for a deader (or pair) to pass, and then shuffle over to the next hiding spot. The geeks were flowing past us, and more and more were starting to yip and yap their whooping coughs as they converged on the grocery store that we'd so recently fled from. For just a second I thought we'd made it past the worst of it when a yelp erupted from a pair of deaders that were just on the other side of a minivan in front of us. Frankie and I both dropped straight to the ground like puppets whose strings had been cut. It wasn't that either of us were worried about these two in particular; it was the thirty or forty others in the parking lot that had us both thinking that discretion was the better part of valor.

Unfortunately, I landed hard, and it was a struggle not to let myself slam against the side panel of the minivan, to produce the sound that would surely draw this massive pack of drones towards us. My trustworthy Levi's stopped the skin of my knees from tearing, but couldn't protect my knee cap from the jolt of impact. It was hard not to grunt at the jolt of pain, but I knew that if I did they would hear. Frankie grabbed my thigh hard, urging me to silence as the two deaders started to come around the other side of the van, following the calls of their rotten brothers and sisters.

With their brown, shriveled skin, drawn teeth, and scabrous, oozing bodies, all deaders are disgusting. The pair next to us was exceptional, though. Once again, it was a male and female moving side by side, their vacant eyes focused on where the rest of the drones were yipping and yelling frantically on the other side of the building to the sound of falling trash and metal. Both were shirtless, and the only way I could tell that one was female was from the singular, shriveled tit dangling towards her stomach. The other had been torn off, the putrid skin where it should have been wrinkled and puckered with faded bite marks.

It was in moments like these- and don't be fooled; I've had more than a few- that I always thought of the movie *Jurassic Park.* In particular, it was the scene where the lead scientist had a stand off with a T-Rex and played the "if I don't move, you can't see me" card. But deaders weren't dinosaurs, and while their eyes were milky and blood splattered, they could see you just fine whether you were moving or not. We needed these two to *not* see us. Having them this close, it was hard for me to resist not killing them. A completely reasonable, rational part of my mind was trying to tell me how- if I cut their eyes out- they would definitely not see us. The other part of my mind argued that said action wasn't prudent.

"Get ready," Frankie whispered beside me, his voice barely more than an exhale of breath. The two deaders were moving past us, and Frankie gave a shove to my thigh, the silent signal to move. We shifted around the front bumper of the minivan, and my always stalwart brother was starting to breath heavy.

"Gimme that," I whispered, reaching for the duffle Frankie had over his shoulder. Frankie was strong as shit, and bigger than me by a significant margin, but it wasn't all muscle. He'd been carrying his duffel for the past few hours, and it had only gotten heavier. We needed to move- fast- and Frankie was one of mine. I was fond of him in my own way, and wouldn't allow him to die just because the weight of our supplies was bearing him down. Plus, Lacy would be pissed at me.

"Get off me, pussy," Frankie said in a whisper, his voice still good natured as he slapped my hand to the side. "I got this. We'll trade in a bit, but right now we gotta get out; ain't got time to be shufflin' shit around."

I nodded to him, and we both worked our way around to the front of the minivan, still bent low. We darted back and forth, running and scuttering to any form of cover that we could find. It took a few frantic minutes of "life or death hide and seek," but we reached the main road, ducking for cover behind a dumpster at the edge of the parking lot. If we could push hard, Branberry was only a ten minute jog away. I was just trying to figure out how to make it across the road when luck favored us.

An explosion of hyena barks erupted from the backside of the grocery store that we'd fled from. Entranced as they already were, every deader in the area started to bark loudly. They streaked towards the back of the building, moving faster than you would assume their rigored limbs could go. Just like that, Frankie and I had a clear path across the road.

Needless to say, we booked it; hauling ass down the gently descending slope of Mission street. Frankie was huffing loudly, and I grabbed him by the duffel's strap and hauled him forward, driving him to keep my pace. He managed, his heavy feet moving faster, and I pulled the worn strap from his back when we reached the other side of the street, looping it over my chest as he caught his breath.

"Fuck, Cleet," Frankie gasped, hands on his knees as I shouldered the pack. "Maybe you're right; I need to lose some weight."

I started to chuckle. After all, we were safe now, and that's what you're supposed to do. I had a witty response prepared, but it fell mute on my tongue as my eyes landed on the side of the road that we'd just left; the opposite side of the grocery store that we'd just vacated. Frankie was awaiting my rejoinder, my quick response; that was how he and I worked, after all. When it didn't come as expected, he stood up straight and followed my gaze to the other side of the street to where the drones- of which there must have been sixty or seventy, now- had converged into one pack. They were moving in our direction with the mindless instinct of a band of starving wolves. It was almost easy to dismiss the tiny black body that was bolting towards us as fast as its four legs would allow, trying to stay ahead of the horde.

"What *the fuck* is that?" Frankie asked.

"That," I said with a distinctly uncomfortable swallow, "is a Chartreuse."

I wanted to be wrong, but I wasn't. Sure as shit, the scampering form running in front of the swarm of deader drones was Nancy's (assumed dead) dog. The canine had been gone for the last ten months, and while it had clearly survived, it looked more than a bit worse for the wear. Now, I've read that Scottish Terriers- pound for pound- are some of the toughest, strongest dogs on the planet. If I'd had any doubt about it, Chartreuse was currently proving the assumption correct. The poor thing was emaciated, its black coat grown long and matted. But it was alive, had managed to survive on its own, and was currently hauling ass to keep in front of the deaders pursuing it.

Problem was, it was running straight towards us. With all of those drones following, it was an unfortunate time for Chartreuse to remember the way home.

"Ah, shit," Frankie muttered as the dog darted towards us, the deaders following on its tail at a distance that was gradually getting shorter. The gated entrance to Branberry wasn't much further behind us. Frankie's face went blank, flat, taking on the waxy, lifeless look that he'd worn when he'd first returned home from his final tour in Pakistan. Most people wouldn't have understood what that look signified, but I did.

Frankie had turned his emotions off. He wasn't a person, anymore; he was a machine with a job to do. "What's the move," he said in a toneless voice, spitting off to the side. The terrier had spotted us, and despite its understandable terror, its tail was wagging as it recognized two regular people that weren't going to eat it.

"Take it down," I said. I didn't waste time weighing my options, because there *were* no options. "That thing gets to us, the whole horde follows it. Everything comes straight back to Branberry's front door."

"Copy that," Frankie said, pulling Suzannah up and cranking in his last bolt with a grunt. He dropped to one knee and placed the stock into his shoulder, taking sight across the length of the shaft with one open eye. He drew in a slow breath, and as he exhaled he squeezed the trigger. The trigger pull freed the drawstring, the drawstring loosed the bolt, and the bolt shot out at the trusting little dog that was running towards us.

Frankie's shot was true, and the arrow followed what I could already see was the perfect trajectory to embed itself in the dog's skull. That is, until Chartreuse stumbled a bit and jigged to the left. Instead of putting the dog down humanely with a clean shot to the head, the arrow drove deep into its rear leg, ripping through the fur and tissue with a spray of blood. The dog yelped and spun to the side from the impact, but recovered the way that animals seem to do when they sense that they are at the moment of their death. Adrenaline set into that little body, and the creature continued to run towards us, maybe even faster than before. The swarm of deaders were only fifty yards behind it.

"Shoot it again!" I whisper shouted.

"I don't have any more arrows!" Frankie hissed back, his voice taking on the heat of exasperated anger. The dog was almost to us, and I realized I had to take care of it, now. This might have been a proper time to use my gun, but at this distance with a moving target … Frankie could have made the shot, but I didn't have the skill. There was no time for me to tell Frankie to draw his Glock. I ran forward, my newly decaled bat in my hand.

Despite a wound that would prove mortal, Chartreuse managed to kick it into the next gear and bolted towards me. He had a hopeful look in his big, brown canine eyes. *These are people,* he was probably thinking. *They'll protect me; they'll fix me. I love them, and they love me. Protect your team, and they'll protect you.*

My bat took the hound across the side of the head, right across my new smiley face sticker. The dog gave a shrill, broken squeal, and then his limp body flew to the side in an unmoving lump.

"Shee-yit," Frankie exhaled, letting his crossbow fall on its strap. "C'mon, Cleet; we gotta move."

I regarded the broken black body that lay unmoving in front of me, regardless of the drones that were only thirty yards or so away. They hadn't stopped when I'd put the dog down; no, their eyes were on us, and- having spotted bigger game- started to pick up speed.

"Should I bring him back?" I asked Frankie. "He's got a good five pounds of meat on him."

Frankie gave me a look, a look that I'd never seen before. Frankie, who had smiled and laughed about giving a bag of heroin to Nancy. "What the fuck is wrong with you?" he asked as he turned towards home. "You don't eat your friends."

Frankie started to jog off, and was moving at a better pace now that he'd had a moment to catch his breath and rid himself of some of the gear. I shouldered the duffle holding our supplies, humming to myself. I'd gotten my rush today, after all. We had a fight coming, and time was short. But I couldn't deny the excitement in my breast.

Don't worry; be happy. Today was going to be a good day.

"Lock it up!" I yelled as loudly as I could as Frankie and I dropped over the wall to the inside of Branberry. There were only a few people out: Lew, talking with Sister Tracy in the middle of the road, and D'wayne, still working on the car. All heads turned our way as Frankie landed heavily behind me with a grunt.

The retired nun and mechanic looked confounded for a moment, but Lew caught the dire tone of my voice. His eyes widened in alarm, and he started towards us in an uncoordinated, gangly jog. He was a smart guy, but had never been overly coordinated. On his best day, he'd always looked like Pinocchio after the strings had been cut. Sister Tracy was quick to follow, and as much as I didn't like her, I was forced to admire the old broad. Her wrinkled face hardened in determination as she walked behind Lew with firm steps. Despite the times, she still found a way to work a stiff crease into the legs of the worn khakis she donned everyday. I couldn't tell you how she did it, but I also didn't care. D'wayne was the only one that lagged, tossing a rachet off to the side as he rose on rusty joints.

"What's happening?" Lewis asked as he trotted up to us. His eyes glanced off of the dead dog that was dangling from my hand- tilted his eyes to me, briefly-but didn't say anything. He either didn't recognize it, or didn't care. Meat was meat, after all, and he could tell by my urgency that we had a larger meal on the table.

"Drones," I said, panting. It wasn't the heavy breathing of exertion like Frankie; no, mine was more of anticipation. There was a certain level of trepidation to be sure, but at the end of the day, I'm an Exterminator, and I lived for this shit.

"Lot of'em," Frankie gasped as I shrugged the duffle off. Sister Tracy stepped forward and picked it up, pulling the strap over her shoulder.

Despite her small stature, she hefted it easily. None of us tried to discourage or take it from her. At one point or another, she'd made us all aware that she was perfectly capable of doing things herself. Even Frankie generally doffed his cap respectfully when the Sister made "suggestions."

"I'll put this on your porch," she said in her no nonsense voice as she turned to walk away. It wasn't the type of nun voice that told you God was kind; it was the nun voice where you anticipated a ruler cracking your knuckles to follow. "When I get back, I expect to hear concise details. Get your jibber-jabbering done while I'm gone."

"She's just *mean,*" I said, my eyes on her departing back, not realizing I'd spoken the thought aloud until Lew snapped his fingers in front of my face.

"Focus!" he said, swerving his head until his eyes were in line with mine. "What's the count?"

Lewis's face was blank and intense. I knew him well enough to know that my childhood friend- my only friend- was gone, right now. *This* Lewis was the one that had been appointed the leader of Branberry; the one that had organized everyone and convinced us to work together. *This* Lewis had no time for joking or palaver. Now was the time for facts, and our survival depended on everyone knowing as much as possible.

"Sixty, at least," I said. "All drones."

A slight widening of the eyes was the only thing that gave Lew's shock away. Sixty drones was bad news, and he knew it. Drones were a give away to the actual size of the main body of geeks. I considered telling him about my odd encounter with Used to be Pretty, but decided to hold off. My suspicious concerns could wait until tomorrow. We needed to deal with the current issue at hand.

"Where's the pack?" Lew asked, still all business.

"Dunno," Frankie said, still fighting for breath as he rearranged his crossbow to sit more comfortably. "Didn't see a full pack, but we heard both of 'em."

"Both?" Lew asked. His eyes flicked back to Suzannah, and his brow furrowed as he went off on an angry tangent. "You weren't supposed to bring that fucking thing!" he barked.

"Yeah," I agreed, speaking up, distracting Lew from his ire and getting him back to task, "two of them."

We were weren't able to delve any deeper into the briefing as a half manic, heart broken shriek erupted from the side.

"Nooooo! What did you do!"

Ah, shit; here we go, I thought, turning my eyes to the home of the only addict besides myself that lived on Branberry. Nancy came bounding down her driveway, moving stiffly and clad in a tattered blue nightgown that had seen many years and better days. Even in the short few hours that we'd been gone her skin had grown more pallid. Her cheekbones were shadowed, and the perspiration at her hairline was thicker. Her fevered eyes were wide and manic, attached to where I held the dead Scottish terrier in my hand. She began shrieking in a strident voice before she even reached us.

"That's my Chartreuse! You killed her, why did you kill her, you kill everything, you're horrible, *horrible*!" she wailed, collapsing on her knees in the middle of the asphalt road where our little group had gathered. She threw her head back, wailing at the sky in anguish. Lew's visage cracked for a moment as he turned heated eyes my way, lips compressing.

"Get Larry-" I started to say to D'wayne, but Lew cut me off with a venomous look that could have felled an elephant at twenty yards. My best friend turned his attention to the soiled mechanic, the anger washing from his face as he replaced it with the congenial expression he adopted when trying to calm/ convince someone to do something.

"Do me a favor," he told D'wayne in a congenial, business-like manner. "I need your help, right now. Bring Nancy to Dr. Larry. Ask him to give her something that will calm her down. Tell him I said it was okay."

D'wayne cast a look at me, but gently lifted Nancy from the broken asphalt and guided her to the house that Larry and I shared. Nancy sobbed on his shoulder, and I wondered if the tremors of her body were from the sight of her dead dog, or her body calling out for her meds. Lewis gave me a scathing glance, but didn't say anything more. We'd have words later, but now wasn't the time and he knew it.

"Will they come here?" he asked, going back to business.

"Yes," I said at the same time that Frankie replied "Hell yeah."

"How long?"

Frankie and I looked at each other, trying to gauge the time and distance. We mumbled back and forth for a moment before deciding:

"Five, maybe six minutes. They'll be circled around the desert side in no more than ten."

I could see Lew's shoulders tighten as he thought things through. Our differences had always been many, but there was none wider than the fact that I welcomed physical confrontation while Lew abhorred it. He held his social position through leadership. He could rally people, calm them, and make the hard decisions that sometimes needed to be made. But there was no denying how much he hated what was coming.

"Sister," he said calmly as the wizened nun returned to us. "Get the sheep to the pool, please."

As much as it may have sounded like it, Lew wasn't speaking in code. He was being completely literal. The pool was just that: a drained, ten foot deep pool that sat in the backyard of one of the vacant homes along our street. I admit to more than a little bit of pride that the concept had been my idea. Not to say that I was some sort of strategic genius; the concept had come from "American Gladiators," a show I'd loved as a child. The basic ideat had spawned from the "Joust," and I turned my eye to a neighbor's greening pool. If we got rid of that stagnant water, we'd have a helluva …

After draining the pool, we'd constructed a stout pillar in the center. It was as sturdy as D'wayne could design it, and rose to a supported platform roughly fifteen feet in the air. The concept was that the drained pool would act as a pit that the deaders would fall into, and the platform was too high for them to reach. They could mill around as much as they wanted, but once the ladder was pulled up they had no way to get to the sheep perched on top.

The term "sheep" had dual meanings. The first time it had been used it had come from Sister Tracy, meaning the lambs under the care of that grand ol' shepherd in the sky. The second meaning was unspoken, but it was a more literal term: those that couldn't defend themselves, let alone anyone else. It was the term for our remaining children- Avery, Bree, and Troy- Nancy, D'wayne's wife Cecille, Lacy, Lew's lesbian girlfriend- Jamie? Janelle?- and a handful of others that would just be in the way. We'd tried to get Sister Tracy to go there as well, but the old nun would have none of it. We'd all agreed on a compromise of her acting as an intermediary. She would gather everyone, get them them to the pool, and then hold her position as a final sentry on the ground.

Tracy gave a curt nod to Lew's ever so polite command, shooting me a cold glance before turning to go gather the others. Her knees moved stiffly with her advanced age, but that didn't stop her shambling gait as she shuffled briskly from door to door, knocking. We'd practiced this drill before, and it wasn't long before we had every single member of Branberry mingling in the road. After the past year, there were just over a score of us left. Organization asserted itself rapidly, and Lew looked at me with stern eyes.

"This is your show, now," he said. "You got this?"

I nodded, but rather than be pacified, he glowered. He seemed even more stern, more worried. God, he was a pussy sometimes. "Don't bullshit me-" he began, but I cut him off.

"I've got this," I snapped, trying to sound calm and confident while I fought down my eagerness. "You take care of our people, then get to your spot."

Dopamine, Dozers, Dogma and Drama

"Get in position!" I shouted out, not that it mattered. We didn't have time for it to matter. I've read that every battle plan lasts until the first arrow is fired, and our first arrow was fired several hours ago.

The drones- close to a hundred, now- were pressed against our gate and walls less than a minute after we'd climbed up to our stations with weapons in hand. There were only a half dozen of us to hold the perimeter: me, Frankie, Jordan from down the block, D'wayne, and a few others. Lew was standing atop Lacy's house with a set of binoculars to track the movement and shout out warnings for where we needed to go. We all knew our positions, knew what we had to do, but we trusted in our walls more.

I took the lead section- *my* section- a twenty foot expanse at the main gate. The roads acted like a funnel, and this was where the deaders would be the most numerous until they found their way around to the desert. I was holding the point guard position in between Jordan and Frankie. It wasn't hard to see that Jordan had yet to forgive my brother in law for the crossbow incident, and despite the deaders on our doorstep he still managed to shoot Frankie the occasional venomous glance. Jovial and irreverent as he normally is, Frankie was all business, now, and didn't even notice.

We were as well armed as we could be, given the time. Each of us had a firearm, but even in this scenario they were still a last resort. Frankie had even spared a half minute to dart back into his house, emerging with an assault rifle hanging from his back. I could make all the jokes I wanted about him being a hillbilly Rambo, but that thing looked *mean,* and his hands curled around it with the familiarity of an old lover.

Our walls were still our first line of defense, but we'd armed ourselves with things that were silent: crossbow, bat, long handled axes, metal poles. Now more than ever, we had to be silent, and we used anything heavy that we could strike a deader down with. After all, the tallest deader in the world couldn't get over our walls very quickly, and we had the time to dispatch them.

But in the handful of attacks that we'd faced in the last year, we'd never had a pack- let alone a group of drones- this large. Out of the corner of my eye I saw Lewis break his face away from the rims of his binoculars to wave an arm high over his head to the street which neighbored ours, the one that Martin and his group lived on. The attack began right after that.

They crashed against the walls and gate with mindless fury, barking and coughing as they slammed themselves bodily against the barrier. There were dozens of them, each uglier than the last, with faces full of hatred and hunger. We walked the edges of the perimeter in our zones, each of us only inches away from their grasping fingers as we dispatched them as quickly as we could. Not every shot was a clean strike. We batted away fingers and hands more often than not. But my bat never ceased swinging as I moved and ran along the distance of my zone. I'd take a few down, and then run over to reinforce Jordan or Frankie. They in turn would return the favor and do the same for me when I needed it.

Even above the gurgling growls that surrounded us, I could still hear the sharp twang of Frankie's crossbow every thirty seconds or so. Jordan's rusty ax- the cheap, plastic handled kind that you bought at knock off hardware stores- was moving almost as much as my bat was. But the black man's face was tightlipped, and I could tell he wasn't enjoying the commotion nearly as much as I was.

I felt *alive,* joyous, even, as I cracked knuckles and jaws, hands and craniums. Despite the danger and imminent threat, this felt *amazing.* I found myself humming my happy song, and the yellow smiley face decal on my bat was covered in putrid gore by the time I ended the first stanza.

"Cleet!"

I heard Frankie's call, and the near panic in his voice cut my exuberance short. I looked his direction to see him backing away from his position and striking out with a heavy length of pipe. The heads of a half dozen deaders were peering over the lip of the wall with milky eyed gazes, gaping and snarling as they reached their arms out Frankie's direction. Frankie carried a lot more weight than I did, and he didn't find it quite as easy to balance on the thin ledge. His thick soled boots were dancing across the narrow cement wall to avoid their grasping hands. I got over there just as he pulled the assault rifle from his back and put the stock against his shoulder, sighting on the nearest one.

I slapped the muzzle to the side with the flat of my hand before he could pull the trigger, and cracked my bat across an arm that was grasping at his ankle. It was a good swing, and connected with enough force that the limb ripped free with a wet squelch, flopping forgotten to the ground. I don't know what had the stolid Marine so spooked, or why the deaders had nearly managed to breach this section of the wall, but- *Yep*, I thought, looking over into the spread of desert that was Frankie's section of the wall. *This is a problem.*

It had only been a few minutes, but my team and I had already brought down a couple dozen deaders. Normally this would have been a cause for celebration, but now it was a problem. Pressed against the walls as they had been, the bodies had fallen atop themselves, one atop the other. The snarling animals attacking us were using the bodies of their fallen brethren as a stepladder to get higher and grip the edge of the wall as they attempted to pull themselves over. There was easily a score of them pressing against the cinder blocks that were Frankie's zone, clambering over one another as they stepped up higher.

"North wall!" I called out, waving my arms at Lew and the others. "North wall! North wall!"

We couldn't afford a breach like this. We hadn't had a deader inside our walls since we first consolidated our boundary. If one or two got in, yeah, that could be handled with little to no casualties. But if we let *this* go- with this many drones around us- we could be overrun in the space of an evening. It was worth pulling the others from their posts to take care of the issue. Avery and her siblings were depending on me to keep them safe. I'd protected them before, and I would do the same, now. My neighbors worked their way towards us as fast as they could, swinging and cursing, sweating and bitching, bashing at anything from the other side that decided to rear up. We were fending them off, but I knew we were in trouble.

I twisted around, cranking hard from the hip as I struck a gray faced deader across the skull. Gray and brown hands clawed at me, pulling at the tip of my bat. There were a few times my balance was precarious at best and I kilted over the wall at an awkward angle, but my smiley face sticker was just as jovial as it had been all day. From the corner of my eye I could see Lew atop his perch, frantically waving his arms at Rocky Coast,Martin's street. I realized that I could hear dim screams coming from that direction. I guess the wedding wasn't going as well as they had hoped.

This could be it, I thought with a fun mixture of eagerness and fear.

There were still scores of deaders along the length of the wall, more than Frankie and I had even anticipated. The carpet of bodies on the desert side was a slope almost four feet high. If they pressed hard now, there was no way that we could hold them back.

To my surprise, they didn't attack though. We'd broken apart the group that had come perilously close to breaching Frankie's section, but the rest of them held back motionless as we all sucked in heavy breaths. One and all, male and female, the scores of deaders held their position a dozen yards away from the wall. This wasn't like them; this wasn't the predictable behavior we'd come to know.

"What the hell?" Frankie said from my side, breathing heavily as he watched the spectacle. D'wayne and Jordan were the closest to us, and they had nothing to say as they gazed out into the desert. Neither did I. This wasn't right.

"*Broomp!*" one of the males barked out, its call echoing across the desert. It was less than a second before a female responded. "*Broomf!*"

"Broomp! … Broomp! … Broomf! … Broomp! … Broomf!"

All of the deaders that were hanging back took up the call, their yapping, coughing cries picking up urgency. It wasn't long before we heard a cacophony of echoing calls from not too far away. Another batch took it up from the other direction, but equally close. The tone of the second group was different, but the multitude of calls was just as large. There was no doubt that the two packs from earlier in the day had zeroed in on us, and- while the distance could be tricky to judge- they might very well be as close as the abandoned grocery store that Frankie and I had taken shelter against. Those of us that were manning the walls looked off into the distance, almost like we were each imagining the swarm of deaders that we couldn't yet see.

"Gosh dammit," D'wayne said despondently, his Cajun twang filled with dread. "T'were fucked, ain't we?"

Everyone drew closer to him in silence, and I used the moment to turn my back to the little group. Sure that I couldn't be seen, I nonchalantly pulled up the sleeve of my flannel to look at my left wrist. Looking back at me accusingly was a half moon ring of teeth marks that had managed to find my skin in the meager space between the wrist of my glove and the hem of my sleeve. I hadn't felt it when it happened, but I sure as shit felt it now. The skin was punctured in a few places, and thick green lines of froth mingled with the bright red lines of my blood.

"Nah," I said to D'wayne, pulling my sleeve back down to hide the deader bite. "We've got this."

The deaders hadn't pressed forward after we'd stopped their initial assault. The minutes ticked by, but the remaining drones continued to hold back, standing in a loose ring around Branberry's wall. They stayed well out of reach, and were slowly growing in number. They continued to bark and yelp, and the echoing calls of the other two packs called back as they drew closer.

There were things that needed to be done as quickly as possible, and we'd left D'wayne up on the wall with his panic whistle. He'd give a sharp tweet on it if things changed. Lewis climbed down his ladder from his perch, and we brought the sheep down from the pool so that we could have a little pow wow.

"Everyone gather up!" Lew called over the worried ruckus of multiple people talking. We gathered around one of the bleach tubs in Sister Tracy's garage. There were several of them, and we'd filled each one to the brim with any brand of bleach we could find. The thirty-one gallon Tupperware containers were makeshift dipping stations, used to kill the bacteria and infection on our bloodied weapons. As long as we kept the totes covered and in the shade to avoid evaporation, we didn't really have to worry about trying to replenish or change them out. It was bleach, after all; the place where germs went to die. I gave a brief thought to plunging my hand into the tub, but knew that it would be pointless. I'd seen it too many times, before; the damage was done, and there was no undoing it. Best to get over it and move on.

Larry was there with us, wringing his hands as he looked everyone over. The pharmacist was a great asset if someone twisted an ankle, or cut themselves making dinner, but there wasn't really anything that he could do if someone came in contact with the virus. He was well aware of his impotence, and the stress of it added to his already jittery demeanor. If nothing else, though, it gave the nervous man something to do, and the people of Branberry felt better knowing that he was there.

"I'm fine," I lied easily as Larry approached me. I felt like I'd been lying all of my life, but you know what they say: practice makes perfect. I was acutely conscious of the burning sting on my wrist as I gave Larry my best smile. *I wonder how long it will take?* The pharmacist took me at my word, and then moved on to check someone else as Lewis threaded his way towards me.

"How do we stand?" my best friend asked me. While he'd started out self appointed, this was one of the characteristics that kept Lewis as the head of Branberry. From his vantage point he'd been able to see what had happened; how things had gone. Moreover, he'd probably been able to see things that we couldn't. But he was still wise enough to look for input from those of us that had been on the front line.

"Ain't lookin' good," Frankie drawled from my side as he took count of the remaining arrows in his quiver. My brother in law was calm and even. When shit got hairy, Frankie was always calm. Say whatever you will about the destruction of civilization, or zombies, or whatever … but those didn't compare to some of the things that Frankie had seen during his tours to the middle east; things he flat out refused to talk about. The tighter a situation was, the calmer Frankie became, which was a good characteristic as far as I was concerned. My patience always wavered when dealing with people that couldn't control their emotions. Lewis nodded, as if Frankie's report had been something he hadn't been aware of.

"Listen up," Lew said, and the worried murmurs around us quieted down. "I know you're all worried, but the situation is under control."

Relieved mutterings filled the garage by those who didn't know how bad things were. Lew held up a hand, and they quieted once more.

"Rocky Coast is gone, though," he continued, referring to the street next to us. "The deaders snapped the hinges on their gate and got in. We've got four people that managed to get onto our side from over the wall, and they're going to need our help. Would you mind taking a look at them, Larry?" he finished, switching his gaze to our bush doctor. Larry nodded uncertainly, his eyes scanning the room and failing to make contact with anyone else's.

"I could use a hand, if you could spare one," he said. "Just in case there's more than I can handle on my own."

While it could have been a reference to having assistance with the wounded, we all knew what he really meant: in case one of them was infected and had to be put down. The pharmacist had never been one to flinch at the sight of blood, but when it came to putting deaders down he could be a bit squeamish. If there was ever a need to mount our walls- such as this one- the pharmacist generally found something to do elsewhere. To the best of my knowledge, I don't think he'd even ventured beyond our walls once he'd taken up residency.

"Take Nancy," Frankie said drily, putting a pinch of tobacco in his lip now that his hands were clean. "She's not doing anything useful."

"Francis!" Lacy said from where she stood near the others. My sister gave her husband a heated look of outrage, but Frankie just shrugged it off as Larry continued to wring his hands nervously.

"Nancy isn't in the best position to assist, just yet," Larry said, chagrined. "I got your orders Lew, and I followed them." He seemed embarrassed. "She's liable to be asleep for a few more hours." *Lucky her,* I thought, and then: *Lucky me.*

"I'll go," Sister Tracy said firmly, her no nonsense attitude as stiff as the crease in her pants. "The Lord's hand is at work, and a shepherd is needed for his flock."

"Thank you, Sister," Lew said gratefully as the nun strode past him. I think I was the only one that realized the gratitude was false and forced, and I smirked on the inside. I had to give him credit; he was a crafty son of a bitch when he wanted to be. Most leaders and politicians are, I'd imagine. Sister Tracy stopped next to Lew's girlfriend- Jamie? Jalinda?- and touched her lightly on the shoulder.

"I could use your aid," the nun said sternly, but with an undertone of gentleness that wasn't lost on me.

Pretty and petite, with blonde hair that reached halfway down her back,- Juanita? Jessica?- bobbed her head and followed. Lew pointedly refused to let his eyes follow them. I was probably the only one that knew him well enough to see the slight tightening of his lips, and I barely stopped from shaking my head. I swear, that woman was going to be the death of him. Lew cracked his neck from side to side, a habit he'd used since childhood when he was stressed.

"Lemme talk with you for a minute," he said, gesturing off to the side with a flick of his chin. To everyone else he said "I want three more up on the walls. Everyone else grab your panic packs and lock yourselves in. If you hear the whistle get to your spots."

Lewis had wandered a few feet down the driveway, and I walked over to meet him. I was more than aware of the hidden bite on my wrist. The other residents of Branberry were quickly dispersing, leaving Lew and me in relative solitude.

"How bad?" he asked in a low voice. I just gave a minute shake of my head, letting silence convey the answer. Lew sighed, rubbing a hand over the stubble on his face. He popped his head from side to side once more, but there were no cracks this time. "What do you think?"

I paused, pretending to think things over. He couldn't be allowed to know that there was a part of me that was enjoying this immensely. I was going to be dead within the week, and had already made plans on how I wanted to go out.

"The Dozers," I said. "I'd say take the Dozers out. See if we can clear enough of them out of the way that we can put down the rest. If we hustle and get it done quick, those packs might not be able to lock in on us. We stay quiet, and they might just move right by."

Lewis looked more than a bit skeptical. The "Dozers" were a project that D'wayne and Frankie had put together in their (more than ample) spare time. They'd taken two pickup trucks from the street and welded an angled sheet of metal to the front bumper. In *theory*, the dozers could be driven through crowds of deaders, breaking into them with blunt force trauma as they sloughed off to the side. It doesn't matter what TV said; no amount of deaders could slow 300hp in four wheel drive. The enigma was that we'd never tried them. Honestly, we'd never been in a situation where we had to. It had been nothing more than a project to keep idle hands busy; to fill the spare time and help people feel useful.

"You're talking about opening the gate," Lew said slowly, giving a disbelieving shake of his head. "We've got a couple hundred drones and a pack- no, *two* packs- coming in on us. Does that seem like sound logic to you? Did you lose half of your brain cells since the last time I saw you?" "Key the trucks up," I said calmly, letting his insults roll off of me. They didn't bother me; he was having a rough day and I knew him well enough to see when he was just being pissy. "Put them right at the gate.

The geeks are still hanging back from the walls. We'll shoot both trucks through, one at a time, and then you close up behind us. We can get both of them out; that quick, that simple."

"Oh, yeah?" Lew said, sarcasm and heat filling his voice. "That quick? That simple? Let's say we do this; what happens when the Dozers need to get back in, genius? We have to open the gate *again*, and you're out of your mind if you think they won't be following you."

"If it works," I hissed back, "then there won't be a reason to be afraid of opening the gate, *genius.*"

I stopped and took a breath to calm myself as best I could. Maintaining a calm fascade had always been a skill of mine, but it was harder than normal this time. My wrist itched.

"Look," I said soothingly, trying to start over. "We can get out. Both trucks, pretty easy. We do what we can. If it works, great. If not, we get close to the wall, hop out, and get over. The only risk is leaving the Dozers out there for a few days until we can go and get them."

Lew's lips tightened stubbornly as he shook his head. He stayed this way for a moment, but then his facade cracked. He bowed his head, pressing the heels of his hands against his eyes.

"I'm tired," he said, and I knew he wasn't talking about the day's' events or lack of sleep.

"I know you are," I replied, putting my arm around his waist. He was enough taller than me that his waist was the only place my arm could go. "You've done your part, and you've done it well. But this is my job, remember? You want my opinion? Well, that's it; get the Dozers out."

"Who's gonna be the other driver?" Lew said, composing himself. "Frankie, I guess? God that sounds like a bad idea. He'll be doing donuts the entire fucking time and shooting that damn crossbow out the window at some cactus."

We both knew better, but this was Lew's way of trying to blow off some steam.

"Not Frankie," I said, all seriousness. "If for whatever reason shit does go wrong I want Frank here. You need him. This isn't hand to hand; it's not wet work. I don't need a fighter, just someone that won't get too squeamish steering a wheel."

Lew sighed. "Who'd you have in mind?"

Our options were limited. Of everyone that served a purpose on Branberry, none could be spared to drive the other vehicle. I thought things over for a moment. "Who came over the wall?" I asked.

"Couldn't tell," he said. "I think I recognized two of them. Three females," he said, recounting, "and one male."

"Who's the male?"

"I don't know. I recognize his face, but I couldn't tell you what his name is."

I was forced to recall that Lewis never went outside the walls of Branberry anymore, not for any reason. That's what he had me for, after all. It shouldn't be a surprise that he wouldn't be acquainted with anyone that lived beyond our border.

"Alright," I said, turning to walk to the back wall that ran along the back yards of the houses on the south side of the street; the wall that was a barrier between Branberry and Rocky Coast. Presumably, this is where Larry, Sister Tracy, and- Jeanine? Jennifer?- would be catering to our newest members. "Let's see if any of them want a piece of this."

The gate squeaked open as we walked into the backyard of the house adjacent to mine. Lew walked next to me, checking the slide on his Beretta. I took in the scene quickly as he holstered the side arm. Lewis and I were late arrivals to this party, and between my people and our new residents there were close to a dozen people in various states of composure.

Larry and Sister Tracy were working together to tie a splint to a woman whose arm was very obviously broken. Lew's lesbian girlfriend was rubbing the back of a bawling woman in a dingy white dress that had seen better days. It wasn't the consoling type of rub; it was a "both hands on your shoulders while I caress the back of your neck" type of rub. I resisted the urge to snigger. And people said that all *men* ever think about is sex. The woman in white continued to sob.

The final female was just standing there with a blank stare. Her cheeks were smudged and dirty, and there was a thick swath of bright red arterial blood staining the front of her white shirt. A bundle of yellow flowers hung forgotten in her hand. The single male, I was surprised to see, was none other than Martin, whom I'd spoken with earlier in the day. More surprising to me was the expression on his face when his eyes alighted on me.

"Did you bring them here!" he roared in anger as he stormed towards me with his hands clenched at his sides. There was death in his eyes. It was a look I understood. Martin was bigger than me by a fair margin, but I gave myself better than even odds as I took an aggressive step to meet him. After all; I didn't have anything to lose, right? My clock was already ticking. Lew stepped between us before we could meet each other, arms spread wide to create a space. Martin stopped advancing before I did.

"Stop it!" Lew shouted, shoving me back. "Both of you, stop it!"

Martin relented, but continued to glare augers at me as he began to pace back and forth on the other side of the Lew-fence. Despite my initial aggressive reaction, I couldn't fathom why he was mad at me until I remembered his question: *Did you bring them here?*

"Yeah, Martin," I said with as much condescending sarcasm as I could muster. There was plenty; it has always been a talent of mine. "I brought them here. I scooped'em all up, and just carried them down the street. It was adorable, you should have seen it. Little baby zombies clinging to my back, riding around my legs. We played tag, and hide and go seek, and *then* I invited them over for a barbeq-"

Lewis gave a sharp snap of his fingers, cutting me off, and giving me a heated look that demanded silence. Yeah, he and I would definitely be having words later. I stopped talking but gave Martin a final look that had more than an ounce of snide condescension in it. Fortunately, between my scathing retort and Lew's intervention, the heated air in Martin had deflated.

The poor man slumped down, elbows on his knees as he clutched at his head, fingers curling tight into his shaggy brown hair. I allowed my own aggression to dissipate. Martin was one of mine, now, and he'd had a rough afternoon. The woman in white continued to wail, and I did my best to keep my irritation in check. Seriously; I've never understood why people cry. It serves absolutely no purpose.

"Here's where we stand," I began, but Lew cut me off.

"You've all suffered a tragedy, today," Lewis said, his voice sad and soft; empathetic in a way that I could never force mine to be. "I'd love to tell you that it was all over. Really, I would. But we don't have time for that, right now. We can grieve, but it has to be later. We're all still in danger, and none of us can spare a moment for anything else until that's been dealt with."

Lew, slick bastard that he is, had a hypnotic tone of voice when he put his mind to it. He made eye contact with each of our new members by turn- oddly glancing over Janis? Jorrelle?- and making his words personal. Even the woman with blood spattered across her chest seemed to be paying attention from within the depths of her shock. Seeing that he had their attention, Lew gestured to me. "This is-,"

"We know who your Exterminator is," Martin said, cutting Lew's sermon off as he turned red rimmed eyes my way. The haggard man stood up and took a ragged breath. "Cletus," he said, extending his hand to me. "Sorry about that; wasn't nothing personal."

"It's understandable," I said, clasping the extended hand and giving it a solid one-pump shake the way my father had taught me. Lewis gave me a look, glancing back and forth between Martin and myself. He didn't need to say anything; the look itself was easy enough to read: *how many people call you that?* I just gave him an indifferent shrug. We had more important matters to deal with.

"Here's where we stand," I said, picking up from where I'd been interrupted, "and I'll keep it short. The group that took your street down, they're just the drones. There's two more packs following up behind them, and they're big ones."

The woman in the dingy white dress broke out into a new gale of sobs, burying her face into her hands. Lew's lesbian girlfriend continued to console her. I hadn't even put forth my proposition yet, but I knew that this broken woman wasn't even going to be a considerable option. One down, three to go. Well, two to go; I couldn't see broken arm girl being in any shape to assist.

"We've got to get rid of as many drones as we can," I continued. "If we can neutralize the drones before the packs come into range, then maybe they'll just keep searching and pass us by. We're gonna take two trucks out past the gates and run down as many as we can. I'm gonna drive one; either of you interested in driving the other?"

Martin scoffed out loud, and Lew gave me a look that told me I'd been too blunt in my proposition. I gave a look back that very clearly said "fuck off."

"We're not going out there," Martin said, slicing his hand emphatically through the air. "I just watched my entire street die. Get your own people to do it."

"You're part of my people, now," I said. "You have the same goal that we do: survive. I just figured that at least one of you would want some payback."

"I'll do it," a soft voice said from the side. I looked over, and was surprised to see that the words had come from the woman with blood spattered across her. Even though she'd spoken, she seemed detached and vacant. Her pupils were dilated, and she seemed like she was in the "coming down" stages of shock.

"They killed my brother," she said softly, sending the woman in white into another strenuous gale of that annoying crying. "He was supposed to get married today."

"When was the last time you went over the wall?" I asked. She looked at me with vacant eyes, but there was anger, there. Anger was good. To my thinking, there are only three true emotions that people have: Happiness, fear, and anger. Any other emotion stems from those three.

Anger is the most useful; happiness, the least. The strange young woman still seemed shell shocked, but there was anger in her eyes. I could see it.

"Does it matter? she said.

Nope, doesn't matter at all. Despite what I'd told Lew, even if things went well this was damn near a suicide mission. That worked for me. Even if things went right, just the way I told him, we'd take the deaders out and stay silent and hidden from the two packs converging on us. I knew that I could find a way to die in the process so that none of my people would ever know that I'd been infected.

It was the *samurai* thing to do.

It might sound dumb, but I've always loved movies with samurais. They'd inspired me to try and be more noble than I knew I was. They had a *code*. But there were no more samurais. Hell, maybe I could even take it as a point of pride and consider myself the last. After all, dying to save others? That isn't a bad way to go out.

"Can you drive?" I asked, looking her over. She was slightly shorter than I was, sturdily built, and had the olive skin tone I associated with surfer movies. I wasn't asking if she was *capable* of driving; I was asking if she knew *how*. Her eyes had the age of someone that had seen far more than they should have, but I would have been shocked if she was a day over nineteen. Her eyes snapped up to mine, her dilated pupils constricting sharply. Yeah, I'd been right; there was plenty of anger there.

"Better than you," she said. I nodded, and then turned to Lew.

"Tell D'wayne and Frankie to get the Dozers pulled up to the gate."

Whether you've met one or not, I want you to imagine a Marine or Navy SEAL; any Marine or Navy SEAL. Now, in your imagination, ask them if their preferred vehicle of combat was a 2011 Dodge Dakota. It's probably safe to assume that you'd imagine the Marine or Navy SEAL laughing in your face.

"Of course not!"they'd say, you imagine. "They're not combat ready, not capable, not anywhere near what we would need!"

I think you would've imagined wrong, though. *I* think that they'd look you square in the eye and tell you that they'd take anything they could find to accomplish the mission; anything they thought would get the job done, and they'd mean it with every fiber of their being. That's pretty much where Mackenzie- the new girl- and I stood right now: using what we had to get the job done. Our tools- the aforementioned 2011 Dakota, and a 2009 Silverado- were what we had to work with.

The trucks had been pulled up in line at the gate, parked bumper to bumper as close as they would go. The engines weren't running. Hell, we hadn't even started them, yet. We'd shifted both of them into neutral and pushed them where they needed to be. The noise of their engines were something that we didn't want to risk, and we had to preserve as much of our homemade fuel as possible.

"This is horseshit," Frankie grumped as he lugged up a few gallons of his moonshine to pour into the tanks. He carried the red spouted tubs easily enough, but the sway of the fluid inside still made his gait awkward. I kept my face carefully blank, refusing to roll my eyes. This wasn't the first time that he'd made the argument, but I'd let him go at it until he'd run his course. "That little twat isn't going to be able to hold up. Kick her to the curb. I'm going with you."

"No, you're not," I said with a sigh. We'd been over this already, several times. "I need you here, Frankie. Branberry needs you. We've all done well, but these people aren't fighters. They need someone to lead them when it comes to this type of thing, and you're the only one that I trust. Besides," I paused for effect, "Lacy would have my ass if I took you out there. Yours, too. We both know that this isn't going to be as clean and clear cut as I told Lewis. If shit goes ass up, if I don't make it back," *-which I wouldn't-* "I need you here so that I know that my sister and the kids are safe."

Frankie didn't say anything, and that was answer enough. He wordlessly poured his brew into the gas tank of the Chevy.

"How long do you think that'll last?" I asked, hoping that I'd gotten the point across.

"Hard to say," he grunted after a pause. "It's a good batch; figure about a hundred and ninety-six proof. But these are both V-8's. I've only got enough for a gallon each." My brother in law spat off to the side, cocking his FSU hat up his brow with a thumb. "I'd give'em about a quarter of an hour, considerin' how you're gonna have to run'em; maybe a little under."

I kept my sigh to myself; that wasn't a lot of time, but it would have to be enough.

"Why are you sweating?" he asked out of no where, squinted eyes on me. I swept a finger across my brow to find a slick band of luke warm perspiration. "Just nerves," I lied, suddenly incredibly conscious of the bite hidden on my wrist.

"Bull shit," Frankie said, eyeballing me in a speculative way. "You don't have any nerves, Cleet."

"Well, maybe I do now," I snapped back, feeling my face flush with anger. "Maybe I've never driven some half-assed, jimmy rigged truck out into the middle of a bunch of fuckin' deaders; you ever think about that?"

Frankie didn't rise to my bait the way that he should have. He didn't seem angry at my heated tone. He was silent for a moment, and then let his innate hillbilly fall to the side for the moment as he watched me with a soldier's wizened eye.

"You planning on coming back?" he asked, his southern twang disappearing. In all of those events in Afghanistan that he wouldn't talk about, he'd seen suicide runs before, I'm sure. He knew me well, and maybe he'd caught a scent of what I was really anticipating.

"Probably not," I sighed, my shoulders loosening. I probably could have fabricated some heroic story, but like I said; why lie?

Frankie regarded me for a moment, and then pulled the nozzle of the gastub from the the tank, letting the remaining liquid slosh around inside. He lifted the spout to his lips, and let his home brewed 'shine run into his mouth. He coughed as he swallowed, and then held it out to me. I wasn't one to pass it up. It was liable to be the last sip I ever had, after all. Don't get me wrong; I wasn't afraid of my impending death, but i'd rather not do it stone cold sober.

"Give'em hell," Frankie said with finality, wrapping me in a very masculine "man hug," the type that involved a handshake combined with a one armed hug and much back slapping. I clasped him back, and for once in my life I meant it. I'd always liked Frankie.

"Watch out for our people," I said as I pushed away with my own sense of finality. "And take care of my sister."

The Best Laid Plans

The engines of the two trucks flared to life, and Mackenzie and I peeled through the narrow space of the opened gate as quickly as we could without colliding with each other. Both of us fish tailed, a bit. I'd always loved driving, but it had been long enough since I'd done it that I was a bit rusty. You know what they say about riding a bike, though … or in this case, driving a pick-up.

The shovel head of the Dakota wasn't three feet past the gate when I plowed into the first deader. The walking corpse slammed into the slanted sheet of metal, exploding onto my windshield like rotten fruit before sluicing off to the side and out of my view.

Holy shit, I thought, *it really does work.*

I heard a screech and squeal of tires behind me, and glanced into the rear view mirror to see Mackenzie zooming in on my bumper. I flicked my eyes back to the road and hit the gas pedal. A fender bender was the last thing we needed, right now. The V-8 engine of the Dakota roared to life.

In the relatively short amount of time that it had taken us to get the Dozers set up, the number of deaders had continued to increase, and I hadn't expected the number that I found waiting for me. There were hundreds of them, and it was easy to tell that they weren't all drones, anymore. There were forerunners of the pack, and here and there I caught the considering gaze of one that seemed more alert than normal. Didn't matter to me; I was going to take out as many as I could.

The Dakota was like a living thing beneath my ass and heels, romping and roaring, bouncing and squealing across the road. I couldn't tell you how many zombies I ran through in those first few moments, but it wasn't long before I had to turn on the windshield wipers to peel away the blood spray. Unfortunately, there was no fluid in the pumps, so rather than clean the windows the blades just left greasy smears. Still didn't matter, though; I could see well enough for what I needed to do.

Mackenzie was behind me, but peeled off in the opposite direction. She was doing the same grisly work that I was, and from what I could see out of the rear view mirror, she was doing it well. I hooked a hard right on Mission street as she peeled left to head down Rocky Coast. My eyes were glued through the windshield, but I cast a few flickering glances up to the rear view to track Mackenzie's progress until she disappeared from view.

Even aside from drones, deaders are mindless things, and it worked to my advantage. They didn't realize that the Dakota barrelling through them would run them down; they just saw something moving and went after it. They crashed and rebounded off of the quarter panels, or ran directly into the the angled dozer head before canting off to the side in a mixture of loose slop. It reminded me of the 8-bit video games I used to play when I was a kid, and I'd be lying if I said I wasn't enjoying myself immensely. I knew that my clock was ticking, but *God damn*, this was a helluva way to go out; this was *samurai*.

I'd spent five or six minutes running them down, whipping the ass end of the Dakota around to go back over the same path, before I realized something was wrong. I was on the desert side, north wall of Branberry, whipping and careening back and forth through the dirt and open paths. I couldn't tell you the last time that I'd seen Mackenzie and the Chevy. I couldn't begin to estimate how many deaders I'd run down, but it was only a fraction of the number that continued to dash directly into my path.

That's when I noticed the problem. For every five deaders that I would run down, there was one that hung back. It's not that these particular geeks were just laggards trailing at the end of the pack; no, these hung back with purpose. It was hard for me to miss as I watched desiccated heads and shrivelled eyes swivel to track my progress with each pass that I made. It wasn't wholly uniform, but for the most part they stood in pairs, male and female, well away from wherever I was. It was the same type of behavior that Frankie and I had seen earlier in the day. It was the same as when the horde hadn't swarmed our walls. It was the thing that I hadn't told Lewis about.

It wasn't *normal.*

There was an intelligence in their eyes, a bright gleam of attentiveness that I hadn't seen until this morning. I wouldn't call it *life* by any means, but there was definitely a level of alertness that wasn't the norm. The ones that I was focusing on didn't have the rogue action or mindless bloodlust that the drones were displaying. These were *thinking, considering,* and it was a bone chilling concept to behold. These were the ones that were very purposely moving out of the way of my truck.

The withdrawn part of my mind garnered that if there had been two or three of these things it wouldn't have been cause for concern. Hell, Frankie and I had already taken down a couple this morning, and they'd caused no more consideration than an itinerant thought that their behavior was peculiar. But now there were a couple score of them, lingering back with knowing eyes, staying well beyond my reach.

The Dakota gave a lurch beneath my ass, and the engine in front of me took in an unhealthy gurgle. It revved up in pitch for just a moment, and then began to stutter. I felt the power beneath me seep away as the truck gradually started to slow down. The roaring, high pitched throttle of the engine disappeared completely, and the well worn steering wheel grew stiff in my hands as all the power faded away. The truck staggered to a slow, grinding halt in the sand, and I could already see several dozen deaders converging on me.

I'd never been one to call myself overly emotional, but this in particular was a cold moment of consideration for me. I looked over at the wall that encircled Branberry, roughly a hundred yards away. I reached down and turned the ignition key of the truck into the off position, more by reflex than necessity. I glanced down at the Sig 9mm on my hip. It was for emergencies only- and if this wasn't one, I don't know what was- but the thirteen bullets in the clip wouldn't serve me much, right now. Moreover, the sound of the gunfire would just draw the rest of the packs closer like a moth to a bright light. I snapped the holster open with a click, and tossed my handgun over to the passenger seat. The others could find it later, after everything was done.

I wrapped my hand around the haft of the aluminum bat that was leaning against my knee, sparing a brief glance for the smiley face decal. It grinned at me, and I grinned back as I put my hand on the truck's door latch to step out. I'd just started to tug it up when I heard movement from behind me, from the small half-cab behind my seat. At the sudden sound I whirled around fast enough to give myself whiplash, and found myself staring into the bright green, adrenaline filled eyes of Avery, the oldest child left on Branberry.

"What's that button do?" she asked, voice thready with excitement as she pointed to a random knob on the center console. My jaw dropped open, but no sound emerged.

Shit.

It took a supreme effort, but I crushed down my immediate resentment and irritation for the little brown haired pre-teen.

No! This was my time! I was supposed to die here! I wanted *to die here*!

Rationality reasserted itself quickly, however; there wasn't time for it to do anything else. While it may have been my plan to die with honor- without anyone on Branberry ever knowing that I'd been bitten- that plan had changed the moment I'd realized the little girl had hidden behind my seat. I swallowed down on my bitterness. If anything, I should have been ashamed of myself for not realizing that she'd been there, earlier. My eagerness- my need- had clouded my senses. That, and the high backed front seat that she'd hidden behind.

No time for regret, though. The deaders had reached my trusty Dakota, and were beating themselves bodily against the windows and hood. I estimated that it would take less than a minute before they got frustrated and started bashing themselves against the glass hard enough to break it. That meant that I had less than *less than a minute* to get my little stowaway ready for something that she wasn't prepared for, no matter how much the harsh world had toughened her. There was no question in my mind; she was one of mine, and I was going to get her over the wall and back home.

I grabbed her by the wrist and pulled her bodily into the passenger seat. I'll admit that I may have gripped her harder than I meant to, but there was no time for remorse as I pulled her slender form over my shoulder. She plopped into the seat beside me, limbs akimbo, but her indignant squawk was cut off as I ripped my Sig from under her ass, causing her to cant further to the side.

"Shut up!" I barked, and then continued speaking before I'd even realized that she'd listened. Her lips were pressed tightly together with fickle, pre-pubescent angst. "You stay next to me!" I shouted, checking the slide of the Sig to make sure a round was already chambered. "I don't care what you think, what you see, you stay next to me unless I tell you otherwise. You don't run until I tell you to, and when I do, you get to that God damn wall!"

I flicked the safety off, and then fired two quick rounds through the glass into the skulls of the deaders pressed against the driver side door. All sound was drowned out beneath the eardrum shattering concussions in the enclosed space as the bullets ripped two coruscating holes in the window. Avery might have screamed, but if so, I didn't notice. The bodies toppled to the side, and I opened the door, slithering through the gap and sliding out. I grasped Avery by the scruff of her neck and dragged her with me. My ears were ringing like a dog whistle had been blown into them, but I frantically took in my surroundings as Avery plopped down into the hardened desert sand next to me.

"Move!" I shouted urgently, cracking a deader across the dome with my Happy bat. The strike didn't have my normal conviction since I was wielding it with a single hand, but it got the job done. Avery flinched at the sound, her face going pale. It didn't seem as fun to her now that she was in the midst of it. I could empathize; I would have been having the time of my life if she hadn't been here to distract me with my sense of duty.

We still had a few feet of space as we maneuvered around the blood spattered truck, and while Avery didn't close her eyes when I had to use my Happy Bat again, she did flinch and cover her ears with her hands when I was forced to fire another round off on a deader that had gotten too close. The rational part of my mind was keeping count: Ten rounds- ten *emergency* rounds- left for me to get her back over the wall.

"Move, move, move!" I hissed at her, my eyes locked on the dozen or so deaders that were an immediate threat.

The next few seconds were an odd blur of euphoria and panic, and I don't remember them clearly. In those long, drawn out seconds that lasted less than a minute, I squeezed the trigger of the Sig three more times. I went back to work with the bat in between shots, focused on putting down anything that came near us. Another two pulls of the trigger, and then the aluminum tube was glinting in the fading light once more.

A scream from my rear made me whirl in distracted alarm, at a time when I couldn't afford to be distracted. Avery had followed my hurried instructions to stay by my side, but now, half the distance to the wall (and what must have seemed like leagues of blood filled atrocity and horror to her) she'd broken. Her scream wasn't one of torture, or agony as she was ripped into and eaten. No, it was a little girl's scream. It was the scream of a child that had bitten off more than she could chew, and had finally admitted to herself that she was terrified. It was the scream of the little girl that had broken away from my side to go dashing back to the dead Dakota sitting in the midst of the desert.

God Dammit, I thought with a cold heat, getting ready to dash after her. I'd barely taken my first step when I heard the harsh crack of gunfire. A high pitched whine shrilled past my ear, taking the head off of a deader that I hadn't even seen. I cast a fast, neck breaking glance over my shoulder, and saw the half moon flash of light off of the scope of Frankie's rifle. He waved his arm at me, telling me to make my way to the wall, to get over.

My ears were still ringing, but I heard a telling *thump* from the other direction. I looked away from the safety of the walls, and saw that Avery had made her way back to the Dakota, and had managed to lock herself back inside the cab. Dozens of deader eyes had turned towards the truck at the sound of the door slamming closed. I was forced to evaluate my options as quickly and efficiently as I could, and a few facts stepped forward.

1. Even with Frankie playing hawkeye, there was no way that I was going to be able to get back to the truck, get the girl out, and get her over the wall. Even if I could manage it, if I could fight my way back to the truck with my hillbilly angel on my shoulder, the sun of the day was almost gone, which meant Frankie wouldn't have a clear line of sight; he'd be useless to us.

2. There were enough deaders around me that I had no way of winning; no way of being samurai, either. I'd die if I tried to fight my way through, and that meant that Avery would die shortly thereafter. I could see her in the passenger seat of the useless Dakota, the top half of her face pressed against the window as she watched what was happening. I could see her cheeks bobbing as she sobbed, and then when she began to sob harder as she saw the drones turning their attention on her location.

3. I had only one option if I wanted to save her.

"Hey!" I yelled out as loud as I could, my voice breaking high. "Right here!"

I knew that they couldn't understand my words, but scores of eyes turned my way. Not many moved, though; they wanted the morsel in the Dakota. They needed an incentive, so I pulled the Sig in my right hand, popped a couple rounds into the heads of some of the closer ones, and continued to yell at the top of my lungs, waving my arms as I continued to work my way towards the wall. Aside from those that were hanging back- watching everything with vapid, milky eyes- most of the deaders had turned my way. Most, but not all. There were at least a dozen of them still slamming themselves against the truck. My voice doesn't carry that far, apparently. I only had one- or three, depending on how you looked at it- way of getting their attention.

Bat held in my right hand, I held the Sig towards the sky and fired off my remaining three rounds in short intervals.

PaKaow! … PaKaow! … PaKaow!

I realized it was a stupid decision the moment my chamber clicked empty- those bullets could have gone into other deaders, after all, instead of sailing uselessly into the sky- but it worked. Every deader eye I could spy was focused on me with a lifeless, hungry intensity. The truck had been forgotten, much like when a toddler casts a favorite toy to the side in lieu of something shiny. The animated corpses were moving slowly for the moment, but I knew they'd be moving much faster in a second or so. Now, all I had to do was get back over the wall and hope they followed me.

Kind of ironic, if you think about it; I'd been willing to die out here by myself to help protect my people, but now I had to save my own life while I left one of my own behind. I knew what I needed to do in order to save Avery, and if I wasn't inside the walls to make it happen she would die. I had to leave her in order to save her life, and while it was a bitter pill to swallow it was the only acceptable option that had a chance of success. It was time for me to move, but I pointed a finger to where Avery was still cowering in the Dakota.

"Stay there!" I shouted as loudly as I could, loud enough that it felt like the lining of my throat ripped. I don't know if she heard me or not, but she didn't move. Without another glance I turned and started back towards the wall, wrapping both of my hands around the shaft of the Happy Bat.

Drones were converging all around me, spread out in every direction. There were far too many for me to even consider using my circling trick.

If I was going to succeed, it was going to have to be down, and dirty; straight forward.

I smiled eagerly as I darted forward. This was going to be a challenge.

Neither my bat nor my feet ever stopped moving. I struck at knees, ankles, and hips, only going for the head if it was a clean kill shot. I didn't have time to finish any of them off; there were simply too many. Frankie's rifle barked a few more times, taking out those that had gotten a little too close to my back. I'd thought to wave him off; tell him to stop guarding me. I didn't want the deaders to orient on the sound and resume their assault on Branberry. But then I realized that- if I did manage to reach the wall- they were all following me, anyway.

Huh. Maybe TV was right on that one. Fuck it, then; let him keep shooting. He deserved to have a good time, too, right?

I hacked at the ankles of the two deaders in front of me, and their ankles shattered with the gratifying cracks of a tree branch being snapped in half. Both toppled to the ground, but didn't stop barking and coughing as they attempted to claw their way towards me. The space that they'd occupied gave me a clear view, and I saw that I was only thirty feet from the wall with a narrow, but clear path. I darted forward, sprinting as fast as I could.

"Hurry the fuck up!" I heard Frankie yell from his position.

I couldn't respond. Not because I was too out of breath; no, I couldn't reply because my eyes had focused on the wriggling mound of fallen deaders stacked in front of me at the base of the wall. The limp bodies sloughed to the side as a lone deader stood tall, hacking black spittle as it gave a loud *"Broomp!"* It took less than an eyeblink for me to realize that this was one of the more alert ones, and the back part of my mind noted that it had been intelligent enough to work its way towards the wall and hide itself within the mound of dead bodies.

Bald and brown, putrid and stinking with decay, the male was taller than me by close to a foot. It hissed at me, and part of me was horrified to realize that- in my current position, with my current momentum- I didn't have time to get my bat up in defense or change my trajectory.

Once again, I found myself with only one option. I let my Happy bat fall to the desert floor as the deader swiped a claw at me. The hand sailed harmlessly over where my head had been as I ducked down and barreled forward.

My shoulder slammed into the male's hips as I wrapped my hands behind its knees, pulling forward. Dessicated or not, the man had been huge in life, and was still big as a deader. The towering corpse had about seventy pounds on me, and even with the adrenaline coursing through me I shouldn't have been able to budge him from the ground.

I did, though, hoisting him up easily and tossing him over my shoulder like a bump-man in a professional wrestling circuit. The giant tumbled awkwardly through the air before landing on his head. The dry desert ground was unforgiving, and I heard a satisfying crack as his neck broke and the body flopped to the side. I stumbled to the side from the effort, and looked up to see Frankie leaning out over the wall and holding a hand out to me.

"C'mon, Cleet!" He yelled, stretching his fingers down. "Move!"

"Can't," I panted breathlessly as I regained my balance. I couldn't risk letting Frankie touch me. My brother in law's hand was bare. He'd removed his glove from his trigger hand,and my jeans and flannel shirt were covered with the excrement of the deaders that I'd put down on my suicidal dash towards the wall. Even if I would have allowed the contact, I was tired from the rough exertion. There was no way I could get high enough to pull myself over the wall.

It wasn't hopeless, though. I cast my eyes towards the base of the wall, where the deaders that had attacked us early had fallen in a mound. The pile was close to three feet high, and would work well as a stepping block. I dashed over, clambering up the mound of corpses that had finally decided to die. My stolen, expensive shoes slipped and squelched beneath my heels as rotted flesh peeled away beneath their tread, but I managed to get to the highest point, putting the lip of the wall a mere foot beneath my chin. I jumped, slung an elbow over the top, and ran my feet against the wall until I could throw a leg over the edge and hoist myself over.

Unfortunately, my endurance was shot and I couldn't maintain my balance. I fell over the other side.

The eight foot fall was short, but somehow incredibly long. Fortunately, I landed flat on my ass rather than my head or back, and was only punished with a sharp burst of pain that erupted its way up my spine like a firework. My breath exploded out of my lungs from the sudden agony.As I lay gasping, trying to force the air back into my lungs, I heard a crunch of gravel near me as Frankie's boots hit the ground.

"Stay still," he said urgently as he ran over to me. "Don't move."

"I'm fine," I replied through gritted teeth as I started to stand up. I was rewarded with a dazzling burst of pain at the top of my butt, and a distant voice in the back of my head calmly informed me that the fall had broken my tailbone. It hurt- a lot- but was somehow … manageable.

Besides, who listens to little voices in their head? People like that are just crazy. Seriously. I gained my feet and took a few cautionary steps. I had to limp, but it was doable. I could manage.

"You need to sit the *fuck* down!" Frankie barked. "Now, Cleet!"

I didn't like the tone of his voice, and sudden anger began to build in me. Nobody tells me what to do. Not Lewis; not Frankie. I looked at him, and for a brief moment considered ripping his throat out. It was a funny realization. Outside of wanting to strangle him on occasion- in a friendly way- I'd never had any inclination to hurt my brother in law. I liked the guy. I was mystified by my sudden animosity towards him. Something in my facial expression must have changed, or he'd seen my thoughts in my eyes, but Frankie drew back, his chin twitching to the side as he watched me with sudden apprehension. Fortunately, neither one of us was forced to respond as Lew ran over, D'wayne and Martin trailing behind him.

"Avery's in the truck," I announced before any of them could say anything. Frankie continued to eye me in a speculative way. I ignored him, choosing instead to rip off my filthy and infectious flannel shirt.

Buttons popped off as I tore the breast open, but it didn't matter; the shirt was ruined anyway. I started walking towards my house at the end of the street, doing my best to ignore my limp and walk normally. I knew what I needed to do, and the first step of my plan started at home.

"We know," Lew said, drawing up on my right side. Calm as he normally is, I could see the flush in his cheeks, a sure sign that he was close to panicking. "We were watching. What do we do? We can't leave her there, can we?"

A dark suspicion bloomed in my chest, baring its invisible fangs at my best friend. Something about the way that he'd asked the question- *We can't leave her there,* can we?- had the tones of polite society while asking permission to do just that. I shook the macabre thought off. Now wasn't the time to allow myself to grow paranoid over a slight inflection of voice. Paranoia, much like voices in your head, is for crazy people.

"We're not going to," I said, forcing myself to accept that I had to limp at least a little bit as I walked up my curving driveway. "But we need to move, fast, if we want a chance of getting her back. Where are the others?"

"Everyone's holed up," Frankie said from where he walked on my left side, his aggressive looking assault rifle still clutched in his hands, barrel pointed towards the sidewalk. "We got the whistles out,"- I noted the silver noisemaker swinging from the lanyard around his neck- "and the sheep know to get to the pool if we give the call."

"Mackenzie?" I asked. I'd like to say that I was truly concerned about her, but truth be told I almost didn't care. Yes, she was one of mine, now, but she'd willingly chosen to go on the same suicide run that I had. It was nothing more than a fluke that I'd come back; maybe she'd had the same chance luck. If nothing else, it was polite to ask.

"Came over the wall about five minutes ago," Martin voiced, speaking up for the first time. "She went down Rocky Coast, ran down a bunch of those fuckers, and then pulled up next to the wall." Martin gave me a withering look that still had a fair amount of heat to it. "She wasn't stupid enough to wait for the truck to run out of gas. She's with your nun."

"Speaking of gas," I said, ignoring my mourning neighbors comments as I turned to D'wayne, "do we have any left? The old stuff?"

I was referring to the stores of fuel that we'd pilfered from abandoned vehicles in the early days, back before we learned that rancid gasoline would clog and rot our engines. It took D'wayne a moment to catch on.

"Reckon we do," he said slowly, voice twanging in that *N'Alin's* style. "Twenty, m'be t'irty gallons, or so."

"Good," I said, stopping before the front door of my house. "Get some buckets, pitchers, whatever, and start pouring it over the walls onto the deaders we put down. Then we light 'em up."

Lewis stopped flat in his tracks, gazing at me with an expression that was just short of slack-jawed.

"Are you shitting me?" he damn near shrieked, if a shriek could be constrained to a near whisper. "You want to light a fire against the walls?" My best friend shook his head in exasperation, like I'd reached some new level of idiocy that he simply couldn't fathom. "Don't you think," he continued, voice dripping sarcastic scorn, "that that might compromise the structural integrity, just a bit?"

I let his acidic tone roll over me. Yep, he was definitely panicking, now, although he was hiding it well.

"It's concrete, Lew," I deadpanned, "reinforced with rebar. Last time I checked, cinder blocks don't burn, and- quite frankly- the walls are already compromised. They've almost gotten over once already, climbing on the ones that we put down earlier. Shit, man, you saw how I got back in. How long do you think it'll be before the piles are big enough for them to walk right over the walls? It's not a perfect solution, but I'm buying us some fucking time!"

I realized I was yelling- something I wasn't prone to- and bit down on my tongue to stop the tirade. Lew's lips tightened like he'd bitten into something sour, but he didn't have an immediate response. I took a calming breath.

"Get the gas. Pour it out. Drop a match," I said in a much more level tone, but I couldn't stop my eyes from drilling into his. I realized that I was being much more confrontational than I normally would be, but given the circumstances I deemed it acceptable. "We light the bodies, and those other sonsabitches will come towards the light- *praise Jesus*- and burn up right beside them."

The silence hung heavy for a moment, interrupted only by the calls from the deaders beyond our territory. If anything, Lew's face grew harder and more bleak.

"Do it," he said after a moment that stretched forever, his lips twisted with distaste. It seemed like the words were being torn from him, but he nodded to Martin and D'wayne, who started to move off with haste.

Yeah, you're gonna do it, I thought to myself. *Why the hell were you waiting for him to give you permission? I already told you that this was what we were going to do.*

Lew waited a moment, his eyes on their departing backs, before turning once more to me. He took a step closer, and when he spoke his voice was pitched low.

"Is this really worth it?" he asked once D'wayne and Martin were far enough away that they couldn't possibly hear. He might as well have been yelling as far as I was concerned. The dark phantom of suspicion reared its head once more, but this time I knew it wasn't paranoia. I felt my molars grinding together. I knew what he was asking, but I wanted to force him say it out loud.

"Is what worth it?" I asked in a light, innocent tone as I continued to glare augers at him. He knew me as well as I knew him, and I had no doubt that he recognized the expression on my face. He knew that look, and I could see him wilt a little bit with guilt. He knew exactly what I was forcing him to, and it didn't sit easy with him. He shuffled his feet, looking uncomfortable. It was a moment before he spoke, a moment more than we could afford.

"It's only one," he said under his breath, like the damning shame he felt compelled him not to use his big boy voice. He wouldn't meet my eyes. "You want to risk all of us, just for one?"

A fountain of rage exploded through me, hot enough to burn stone. By some miracle I managed to hold it in, although I felt my face go slack as I limped towards him until we were almost chest to chest. I spoke into his ear, my mouth uncomfortably close to his chin.

"I'll open the gates myself, and let those things in here to kill every one of us," I hissed softly, "before I leave her out there. She's one of mine. Don't test me on this, brother."

In his defense, Lew at least had the decency to look abashed as he wordlessly turned to walk away. "C'mon, Frankie," he said over his shoulder to where my brother in law stood silently on the curb. My sister's husband had stayed so quiet that I'd forgotten he was there. "We need to get to work."

"Nah, I'll catch up in a sec," Frankie said, disregarding Lew's command with utter indifference. "Gimme a moment; I just wanna check on Cleet, real quick. Hard fall, and all."

Lew didn't argue or cajole the insubordination, a sure sign that he felt a modicum of guilt, like a bad dog caught digging through the garbage. He just gave a shameful nod and then walked off.

"I don't have time," I said urgently, turning to put my hand on the doorknob. "I need to talk with Larry."

"Oh, I think you got time for this, Cleet," Frankie said, and the flat tone of his voice caught my attention. I turned around, feeling wary. I couldn't tell you the last time that I'd felt wary- truly wary- about anything. Frankie, my happy, jovial, hillbilly brother in law was staring at me with blank eyes, a plug of his chewing tobacco bulging from his lower lip. My eyes alighted on the protrusion from his jaw, and for just a moment a stupid conversation we'd had a few months back flashed through my mind.

Seriously, Frank, that shit is disgusting.

Stop being such a pussy. This is man shit, right here.

Man shit? You're out of your mind. You spit that garbage everywhere.

What do you expect me to do? he said with a laugh. *Swallow it?*

You strike me as a swallower, I chuckled back. *Don't be a slave to your addiction.*

I had expected a cutting rejoinder, but when I glanced over Frankie hadn't looked amused. In fact, he'd looked grim. He'd looked at me for a moment, his face unreadable, and when he spoke his good ol' boy accent had fallen away.

I do it to remind myself that I'm a man, and that sometimes men have to do hard things; things that they don't want to do, but need to be done. I do it to remind myself that I'm tough enough to do those things, whether I want to do them, or not. Besides, he'd said with a wide grin that hadn't reached his eyes as he drawl returned in full force, *you ever known a tough country boy that didn't like a chew now and then?*

The memory flashed through my mind just before Frankie said "I notice you got a little hickey on your wrist, there."

The casual way he said it may have sounded conversational to anyone else, but I knew him, and didn't miss the way that he was clutching his assault rifle. His words didn't sink in at first, but then realization slowly dawned.

I'd taken my flannel off. Frankie had been walking on my left as I limped towards my house. The deader bite was on my left forearm.

God damn it; I didn't even think about that. How stupid can I be? So much for not letting anyone know about it.

"You noticed that, huh?" I asked in the same conversational tone, pretending that a patch of weeds in my front yard had caught my attention. "What were you thinking about it?"

It was utterly absurd. With everything else that was going on less than a dozen yards away in every direction, Frankie and I were having a calm, passive- aggressive conversation regarding the fact that I'd been infected and we both knew it. I looked at him, awaiting his response.

Waiting for a bullet in my head.

"Don't quite know what to think, just yet," he said, spitting off to the side. His hands never strayed from the placement on his rifle, though.

"I'm fine," I said curtly, urgent to be on to the next step in my plan to recover Avery, and hoping to draw the conversation to a close.

"Nah, Cleet," Frankie drawled, "I don't think you are. See, I was there when you tumbled over that wall. I watched you hit the ground, and I heard something in you break. I don't know what it was, but to my way of thinking, you shouldn't even be able to walk right now. But hell; here you are. So what do you reckon I'm supposed to think about that?"

Despite the civility we were showing each other, it was a terse moment with a lot hanging on the outcome. I took a moment to think, choosing my next words very, very carefully.

"I think," I began slowly, "that we have more important things to worry about, right now. I *think* that I told you I'm fine. I *think* that this is something we can talk about tomorrow."

"Uh-huh," Frankie said, unconvinced. "Assumin' there is a tomorrow."

"There will be," I said, grim with certainty. "I'll make sure of it."

"Why?"

"Because this is the only thing I've ever been good at, and I know what I'm doing."

I watched something break in Frankie in that moment, some stalwart wall that he always held firmly in place. It was just a twitch that most people probably wouldn't have even noticed, but to me it revealed his indecision and anguish.

"How the hell am I supposed to handle this, huh?" he asked, his voice venting the emotions that his face wouldn't show. "What if you turn?

You're going to. We both know it."

"I won't," I replied, knowing it in my aching bones and body.

"Yeah? And how's that, exactly? There's only one way this story ends, Cleet."

He was right, and we both knew it, but I didn't have time to concern myself with it.

"Because I won't let myself," I said with resolve. "I'll fight it every inch of the way." I took a slow, deep breath. I hated myself for what I was going to say next, but it had to be done. "Look, I asked you today, I trusted you, to take care of Lacy. I put that faith in you. I'm asking you to trust me, now. I know what I'm doing."

"And what is that, exactly?" Frankie asked. "We've been jaw-jackin' for a few minutes now, but you still haven't said what it is."

"I'm going to get Avery home. Once that's done and we've made it through the night, we can bring this little matter back up. Can you give me that much, at least? At least until she's back?"

Frankie thought it over with a stone face. It was a tense few seconds; seconds that we couldn't afford to spare. Frankie would never admit it, but he loved those kids just as much as my sister did. I'd never say it out loud, but maybe I did, too.

"Yeah," he said after a moment, his hand loosening from around his rifle. "What are you gonna be doin' while we pour gas on a bunch of corpses?"

"I'll be getting a distraction," I replied. A band aid had been placed on the issue for the moment. It wasn't permanent, but it would hold for now. I gave him a nod and turned to walk into the house. "A distraction?" he called. "The fire ain't enough?" *Nope. Not for what I have in mind.*

"Don't worry about it," I said instead as I opened the front door and stepped inside the peaceful dimness of my entryway. "Just get that fire lit. I'll take care of the rest."

I closed the door before Frankie could answer, reveling in the comforting silence and shadows. I knew what had to come next. I didn't want to do it, but I'd never been one to shy away from my duty. Pondering what I was about to do, I missed my Happy Bat terribly. Good thing I had another one.

Pills clickety-clacked against each other inside clear orange prescription bottles as I shuffled through the shelves that held the assortment of antibiotics, antidepressants, and anti inflammatories that Branberry called its pharmacy. None of it was what I was searching for, though, and I huffed in irritation. It was too dark to see clearly, so I put down the dead weight of the black plastic trash bag in my hand and picked up the battery operated lantern that sat next to my bed. A quick click of the press top button and, *voila,* let there be light. Finding what I was searching for was significantly easier at that point. I grabbed it from the top shelf and tucked it into my pocket.

"You don't want that, boss," a nervous voice said from my rear.

I looked over my shoulder to see Larry standing in the doorway. The one time pharmacist looked haggard, and the even light of the lantern cast shadows that gave great details to the worry bags that circled under his eyes. The last year or so- however long it had been- hadn't been kind to him. This past day even less so, and it showed.

He'd been a bit skittish when we'd first met him, and had grown more so every day since. By my math, that added up to a lot of skittishness. He never drank, never smoked from the small cache of stale cigarettes we had from a previous tenant, and as far as I knew never delved into the shelves of various medicinal products we had stored in my room. *Maybe he should start,* I'd thought to myself on more than one occasion. *Might calm him down, some.*

The only time that Larry had ever seemed calm and in complete control of himself was when he was treating someone. Didn't matter whether it was a scraped elbow or a broken bone; he was as cool as the underside of a pillow. He'd done well by us, and- quirky or not- I'd never reconsidered or questioned Lew's offer for him to come with us on the day we'd met him. Now he stood facing me with an expression of utter seriousness.

"What type of syringe should I use?" I asked. From the corner of my eye I could see an orange glow gaining intensity from the window. The boys of Branberry- eager or not- had gotten the bodies lit. If it hadn't been so before, time was now of the essence. If anything, it had now become even more of a commodity. Seconds were ticking by while Avery sat in that dead Dakota. "Twenty gauge?" I asked, referring to the bore size of the needle. "Twenty-two?"

"You don't want it," Larry repeated firmly, showing a resolute demeanor I'd never seen him display before. A little part of me bristled, but mostly I admired him for it.

"Relax," I said, trying to make my voice sound soothing, the way that Lew would. "It's not for me. I just want to try something out, and I want to make sure I'm doing it right."

Larry seemed uncertain, like he could hear the lie in my words, but he'd trusted in Lew and me implicitly ever since he'd made the decision to make his home with us. We'd kept our word to him, and he'd valued that. He may have never come out and said it, but his staunch support of our actions and decisions had said more than words ever could. He walked over to a wicker laundry basket that housed a random assortment of medical supplies. After rummaging around for a moment, he emerged and handed me a single-use syringe wrapped in airtight plastic.

"Thank you, Larry," I said as I took the syringe from him and tucked it into the back pocket of the almost clean jeans I'd rapidly changed into. I picked up the black garbage bag and turned to leave, my spare bat in my opposite hand. "For everything."

I'd made it a half dozen steps before he spoke up.

"Are you going numb, yet?" he asked after I'd limped past him. I stopped in my tracks.

"What do you mean?" I asked. I was trying to pretend confused ignorance, but the pharmacist didn't falter.

"You've been diaphoretic- sweating- ever since you got back. You're pale; drawn. Stronger, too, I noticed. I saw when you ran back over the wall; the way you picked that deader up like it was nothing. In my experience, physical numbness is the next thing that starts to set in once you've been infected."

I paused, and in that moment I thought about killing him. Thought about it very hard. Frankie knowing my secret was bad enough, but Larry knowing? The odds of me quietly disposing of myself were becoming more slim. But there was no denying the way that the broken ends of my tailbone were grinding together with every step I took, and how it didn't hurt as much as it should. Moreover, Larry was one of mine, and I had no doubt that Branberry would need him in the next few days.

"How long do I have?" I asked bluntly. *Why lie* seemed to be my mantra for the day.

"Hard to say," Larry said, looking uncomfortable. "Could be two days; could be a week."

"Well, that's plenty of time, isn't it?" I asked, forcing a smile onto my face. "I've got something I need to take care of, so let's keep this between us for just a bit."

Bat in one hand, and garbage bag in the other, I turned and walked out of my home without another word.

How Heroes are Made

The front door glided open with barely a sound as I stepped into the house.

Time was more precious than water at this point, but I'd taken a moment or two before entering to look around the perimeter of Branberry. The flames were rising high outside of our walls, and thick, stinking, plumes of smoke were rising into the black night sky. As I'd predicted, the hundreds of drones that surrounded us- drawn by the light- had started to walk straight into the flames, further fueling them. I hoped with all my heart that Avery had managed to hold out this long, otherwise this dark path I was about to undertake was a waste of time.

I held the door knob curled in my hand so that the latch wouldn't make a sound as I closed it behind me. I'd never been inside this house before, and for a shuddering moment as I raised my lantern high, I was glad for it.

Sculptured, blown glass unicorns sat everywhere. Each wall held at least one crucifix or a picture of Jesus. The bench that ran along the windowsill held an assorted collection of snowglobes. The windows held ruffled curtains, and the couches were covered in fitted, thick, clear plastic sheeting to preserve their cleanliness. Precious Moments statuettes covered everything else. It smelled like old people. It smelled like sickness. It smelled like the urgency of craving addiction.

It smelled like Nancy.

The living room- which could easily have been the set for a rerun of *The Golden Girls* - was empty. The floorplan of the house was the same as mine, and if she'd been in the kitchen I would have seen her. Since it was dark and empty, I helped myself to her silverware drawer, choosing a single utensil.

I'd committed myself to my plan, but that didn't stop me from being overly furtive as I crept down the hallway to the master bedroom. The door was slightly ajar, and I pushed it open. In the even light of the halogen lantern, I could see that the walls of the room were covered in ornate picture frames. Pictures of her dead husband; pictures of her dead dogs in a myriad of fun and adorable poses; pictures of her husband with the dogs; pictures of the dogs in Halloween costumes, in Christmas costumes … You get the point.

Nancy herself was lying beneath a rumpled, frilly afghan, wearing a worn nightgown. While she'd never been particularly sturdy in terms of stature, she looked undeniably frail, now. The house was relatively cool, but the glow of the lantern glinted off the light sheen of sweat on her brow. I was surprised to see that her half lidded eyes were open- that she was watching me- but they had the glazed look of someone still under the heavy influence of her "medication."

"What are you doing in my house?" she rasped. Her voice was weak; her words slurred. Her tone carried none of the frantic urgency and strength that she'd had earlier in the day.

"It's been a rough day," I said, doing my best to keep my voice soothing and level despite the urgency. "I know it's been hard on you, especially with Chartreuse- and I'm really sorry about that, but I had to- so I brought you some of your medication to help." Pause. "I thought you might like it."

While they didn't lose their glaze, her eyes seemed to light up at the notion. She looked at me eagerly as I pulled the wrapped syringe from my back pocket, as well as the spoon that I'd pilfered from her kitchen. A lighter came next, and then finally the small baggie of heroin that Frankie and I had found earlier that day.

I'd been counting on Nancy not being cognizant enough to recognize what the devilish powder was, and she didn't let me down. Her eyes did seem to focus on the word "Jesus" that Frankie had scrawled there in black Sharpie, but then she smiled up at me, her dilated eyes wavering back and forth a little bit at just about where I was. It was beautiful, in it's own sort of way. It didn't make her look younger; as a matter of fact, it highlighted her pallid hue, and the way her skin looked like old parchment.

But it did make her look happy; content, even. She wanted this. I was doing her a favor, and she was grateful for it.

"That's kind of you," she said softly as I took a seat on the edge of her bed. "You know how much I need my medicine. My knees hurt so much …" her voice trailed off, and I realized that she was starting to fall back into slumber. I couldn't allow her to do that, yet. My conscience wouldn't let me.

"Give me a second, Nance," I said sharply in a hushed tone. The snap in my voice drew her back, and she looked at me vacantly, like she'd already forgotten I was there. "Your medicine?" I prompted, looking at her as earnestly as I could. It took a precious second, but her memory returned and she smiled once more, wriggling her way up in the bed eagerly until she was in a sitting position.

While I'd never gone through the process before, I'd seen enough cop shows and Netflix dramas to have a fairly good idea of how it was done. I tapped out a generous amount of the white powder into the bevel of the spoon. I didn't know how much to give her, what the right amount was, and then figured that it didn't really matter. I tapped the baggie a few more times. I flicked the striker of the lighter, and held the flame beneath the spoon. I was slightly disturbed to see that my hand had a slight shake to it. No matter the circumstances, my hands never shake.

The heroine began to bubble and then caramelize, turning from a white powder into a brown fluid that ringed the spoon. I traded the lighter for the syringe, tearing the wrapping open with my teeth, and put the tapered bore into the belly of the spoon. I drew back on the plunger until the clear plastic cylinder held everything that it could.

"We're ready, now, Nancy," I said, dropping the spoon of poison to the floor. "I've got your medicine ready; I just need your arm."

In her influenced state, Nancy didn't seem to recall how much she hated me; how much she'd never trusted me. With her "medicine" in my hand, I'd become her best friend. She held her arm out to me willingly.

Now, on television, you're supposed to tie a tourniquet or cinch around the upper part of the arm. The purpose of this is to cause a constriction of blood flow so that the veins pop up closer to the skin for easier access. Well, Nancy's skin was already pretty thin, and I could see the veins just fine. They were like a finely detailed river on a map. I set the pointed tip of the needle against the largest one I could find, and slid it it. Nancy's skin pierced as easily as butter coming into contact with a warm knife, and she never even made a sound as I pressed down on the plunger.

The effect was damn near instantaneous. Nancy's eyes- glazed over to begin with- began to dilate as her lids drooped. The muscles in her face started to go slack, and her mouth dropped open.

"This is good," she whispered, her voice slithering past her pallid lips as her head lolled to the side. "What is it? Oxycodone? Morphine?"

Something like that, I thought to myself as I pulled the syringe from her arm. I wanted to plant my thumb over the blood beading and leaking over her skin- that's what they do on TV, right?- but then figured that there was no point.

"I brought you something else, too," I said as I saw her starting to slip into unconsciousness.

"W'ass that?" she lisped, her words fumbled. Her body had started to slide down beneath the covers.

For a second, I hesitated. I wasn't looking forward to this part. I glanced out of her bedroom window before answering. The glow of the flames around the wall was still holding strong. Thin tendrils of fire were licking over the edge of our wall. Avery was still out there.

"I brought Chartreuse to you," I said.

"She's dead," Nancy coughed weakly, her eyes closing. "You killed her."

"No," I admonished gently, "she was just hurt. But she's better, now, and she wants to see you."

"Really?" Nancy said softly as she reclined further into her bed, eyes closed. "Can I see her?"

"You sure can," I said, trying my best to sound jovial as I reached down to the garbage bag at my feet.

I pulled the stiff, lifeless body of the terrier out and placed it gently on Nancy's lap. The black legs of the dog were sticking out stiffly, like the post of a mailbox. Dried blood coated its flank where Frankie's arrow had ripped through her, and her squash sized skull was half caved in. Nancy didn't notice, and started to rub her hand lovingly across the coarse black hair, caressing the dead dog and not noticing in the least when her fingers trailed through blood clotted hair. She began to laugh to herself, soft chuckles that barely made their way out of her mouth.

"I missed you," Nancy whispered into the side of her pillow. She smiled vacantly, and I stood up to move over to the other side of her bed. "I love you so much. You scared me, but now you're ho-"

Nancy's mumbled words cut off as I placed her husband's pillow over her face. She didn't really react at first; she just kept petting the dead dog with her fumbling, flopping fingers.

"You're a hero, Nancy," I whispered as I pressed the full weight of my body against the pillow. "You're a samurai. You're going to save Avery, did you know that?"

Nancy's hands had finally stopped stroking the collar of the Scottie, and had begun to paw feebly at my hands. I pressed my body down harder. Her back arched, but it was a weak attempt that I held down easily.

"I could have used a knife," I said as she wriggled beneath my weight, unsure of whether I was talking to her or myself, "or the bat. But that would be murder, and I'd never kill one of my own. We're in this together, all of us, right? You're gonna be a hero, now. You have a *purpose*."

Nancy didn't answer me, and after a few seconds her flailing died down, her hands falling limp by her sides.

I waited a few seconds more before pulling the pillow away from her face. Nancy's eyes- rheumy to begin with- were clouded and gray. At some point, she'd managed to throw up against the underside of the pillow, and the effluence was smeared across her face. I tossed the pillow to the side, and gently lifted the stiff carcass of the dog off of her flaccid breasts, placing it on the flowery comforter of her bed. Gripping Nancy by the wrist, I pulled her up to a sitting position, and with a grunt, hefted her on to my shoulder. Her dead weight wasn't nearly as heavy as I thought it would be, but my nose crinkled as her hip settled next to my chin. Why? Because when people die their muscles relax. This includes the bladder, the urethra, and the sphincter. Fresh piss and shit has a less than enticing aroma.

I'm not a big person, but I'd always been strong for my size, and Nancy weighed much less than I anticipated. I shifted her weight around on my shoulder until it felt comfortable, and then picked up Chartreuse from where she was laying on the bed with my free hand and walked out of the room. It wasn't hard to figure out where the backyard sliding door was; like I said, her house was the same layout as mine. Sliding the door open, I walked out into the backyard. I wondered for a brief moment how I was going to accomplish the next part of my plan, but fortune favored me and I didn't have to wonder too hard.

Nancy, intentionally or not, had been courteous enough to place her patio table next to the cinder block wall that separated the lots on Branberry. It was more than a little bit uncomfortable with my hands full, but I stepped up on a chair, and then onto the table top. From there, I balanced precariously with my load as I stepped up to a Mojave style red clay oven. After that, I stepped up onto the wall with a grunt of effort. Don't get me wrong; I know that I said Nancy wasn't too heavy, but try walking up a steep flight of stairs with ninety pounds of dead weight on your shoulders and tell me how you feel.

My feet were almost in a straight line, like a tight-rope walker, and I stepped carefully along the top of the cinder block wall. The stench of the burning deaders on the other side was cloying, and the smoke burned my eyes and nose, but I continued moving forward until I could feel the heat from the flames flicking over the wall licking at my toes. It was hard to see beyond the bright light thrown up by the fire, but I could see dozens upon dozens of sets of green eyes glowing beyond our borders. I wasn't happy about what had to happen next.

I set the terrier down over my feet, and shifted Nancy's dead weight around over my shoulder until I found my balance. With my free hand I pulled out my panic whistle, placing it to my lips. I took a deep breath, and gave a long, shrilling blow. Even at night, even with the haze of smoke and the light of the flames, I saw scores of glowing eyes turn my direction at the sound. Good. I twisted Nancy around until I got a good grip on her- throat and hip- and then threw her over the wall as far as I could.

To be honest, I didn't think that I would do as well as I did, but her lifeless body flopped to the ground about ten feet from the outside of our wall. The deaders saw it, and almost as one they started to move forward. This next part I found particularly distasteful, but fuck it; I didn't have time to be squeamish. I picked up the dead dog from where it rested on my feet. The little shit may have been the Pale Horse that lead the deaders to Branberry, but there was still a part of me that felt like it deserved better than what I was about to do. I had to be quick, though.

I pulled out my pocket knife, flicked it open with my thumb, and plunged it into the dog's underside just below the breastbone. I wriggled the handle, sawing back and forth, and working the blade down. The stiff bristles of the coarse fur impeded the sawing, and part of me found that very inconsiderate of the dead canine, especially considering the current state of urgency.

Time seemed like it was racing, but it couldn't have been more than ten seconds before I had the dog opened from sternum to stem. Stiffened in death or not, the little black pooch still had plenty of blood and guts to leak and slither out. I tossed the carcass over the wall, over the flames, as far as my arm could fling it. The black body cartwheeled through the air like an overweight ninja star, its intestines spilling out in looping coils as it spun. Chartreuse landed fifteen feet or so past where her owner lay akimbo.

Now I had to move, and move fast.

I jumped down from the top of the wall without thinking, falling the ten feet and landing on my feet in Nancy's backyard. My tailbone screamed in protest, and I staggered drunkenly to the side for a moment, wincing. The pain should have been worse, though, and I knew it. I didn't have time to think about what that implied, but I could hear Larry's words in the back of my mind.

I'd just gotten back into the house, sliding the glass door closed behind me, when I heard another door crack open. The halogen lantern that I'd left inside was still casting its glow, and it clearly illuminated Lew's girlfriend- Jade? Justine?- as she walked through the front door.

"Nancy?" she called out, glancing around towards the vacant master bedroom. "Where are you? The whistle was blown. We need everyone over at the pool."

Her pretty little blonde head swiveled back my direction, and she startled as her eyes landed on me. I saw her. She saw me. Her eyes flicked down at my blood coated hands before looking back at me. Her eyes widened. She drew in a breath. Her mouth opened to scream. Dammit; this is unfortunate timing.

I was breathing heavily by the time I sprinted up to where Frankie and the others were monitoring the perimeter of our flaming walls. As for the pressing matter of time, I figured myself to be way behind schedule. Taking care of Lewis's lesbian girlfriend had required a short period of time that I hadn't factored in, and the clock was still ticking.

It had been awkward for both of us as I wrapped my hands around her neck. She'd fought, clawing at my wrists and wheezing harshly. She was only slightly smaller than I am, and fear had given her a surprising burst of strength.

I didn't help her much, though. I'd given a sharp squeeze, and there had been an audible pop as her windpipe collapsed beneath my thumbs. Her wheezing turned to a high pitched whistle as she let go of my arms and began to claw at her throat, staggering backwards. She tripped over the coffee table and fell over backwards, her legs kicking out in spasms. She passed out within moments.

Great, I'd thought as I'd regarded her comatose form. *Another problem.*

Turns out, it hadn't been too much of a problem at all. Of course, rapid action and problem solving had always been strengths of mine, and the two combined in that moment to give me a simple solution.

It took me less than half a minute to haul her by her wrists to the bathroom and get her into the bathtub. I straightened her limp limbs until she looked peaceful, and then cut her wrists open. I did it lengthwise between the Radius and Ulna of her forearm, the way I'd read you were supposed to do it. She may not have been conscious, but her heart was still beating, and the blood rushed from her wrists in steady spurts, coating and streaming down the sides of Nancy's white bathtub in thick, crimson rivulets.

Suicide. Boom. Problem solved.

Part of me wanted to step back and take a moment to admire my handiwork. I mean, truly, given the circumstances? This had been tuned in, high speed thinking. I'd even finished off the scene by taking- Jassa? Jeanna?-'s pocket knife and dipping the blade into the blood and placing it next to her hand. I mean, seriously, this was art.

Another part of me- the part that I was starting to realize was the infection in my veins- wanted to bite into her thigh. Whether I'd liked her or not, she had great legs, and I thought about it very hard, very quickly. Ultimately, I'd decided that there was no time. Avery was still in the Goddamn truck, and I was behind schedule. I knew that Lew would be upset when he found out, but this was for the best. We'd talk about it, later. Jenson had never been any good for him, anyway.

Martin was at the base of the wall as I drew up and glanced around to take in the situation. Our newest member looked worried and haggard, ready to collapse in exhaustion at any moment. Lew was standing atop the house with his narrow back facing me, watching the movement of the deaders in the desert beyond Branberry's walls. D'wayne was further down the wall to my left, his eyes focused on where I imagined the lifeless Dakota sat. Frankie was up on the wall itself, positioned at a vacant spot where the flames weren't rising. His rifle was still clutched in his hands, and with the light of the flames in front of him all I could see was a black silhouette of shadow. It made him look like Budweiser's finest hillbilly Rambo.

The shadow turned my way, the grim features of his back lit face locking on to mine as I worked my way carefully up the staggered steps of the cinderblock to get to the wall.

"Gimme your sword," I said as I drew even with him, forestalling any uncomfortable questions he might ask. I had my second bat with me, a dull silver aluminum number that I'd used for years, but for what I planned the sword would be better. It'd be quieter.

Frankie looked at me with confusion. Some part of my mind considered that it might have been because he was surprised, shocked at watching me run up the staggered brick wall with relative ease when I'd been limping so heavily such a short time ago. I very firmly told that part of my mind to shut the fuck up.

"Why?" Frankie asked. He was holding the rifle, but his trustworthy ol' crossbow dangled on a strap from his back, and Samantha wasn't too far from his feet. My brother in law's eyes and voice were flat, lifeless, and I realized he'd already assumed the worst would happen and armed himself accordingly: Rifle for long distance. Crossbow for mid distance when his ammo ran out, and Samantha for when it came to hand-to-hand. He had his Glock on his right hip, but I understood Frankie well enough to know that those .45 slugs wouldn't be for deaders. They were a last resort- a quick end- for the people he cared about if things went bad. It was an ominous sight, but if my plan worked right it would never come to that.

"I need it," I said. "I'm going over for Avery."

I didn't wait for his approval. I just reached over and took the sword from where it lay next to his feet. He looked grudging, but let it go.

"Are you out of your mind?" Lewis damn near shrieked from the roof nearest us. Half his face was illuminated by the flickering light of the burning deaders. Maybe it was the putrid stench of the burning, rotten bodies, or the clouds of smoke depriving him of oxygen, but my best friend looked almost manic. I wanted to feel bad for him, but empathy had never been a strength of mine, and- once again- I simply didn't have time to care. His face contorted in fury when I didn't even bother to answer him.

"Here," Frankie said, holding his rifle out to me as he shrugged the crossbow around his shoulder. "Take this."

I shook my head.

"No," I said. "I need you with it. Cross down the wall about fifty feet"- this would put him on Nancy's back wall, where he'd surely see what I'd done, but I had to live with that- "and start taking down as many as you can. I need the noise. D'wayne! Martin!" I barked over my shoulder, "Stay with him on either side! Nothing gets over!"

"I'll go with them," a resolute voice said from over my shoulder. I cast a half glance to see that it was Mackenzie, my partner from earlier. She looked tired, and a bit vacant around the eyes, but still seemed eager and alert enough to do what needed to be done. I gave her a nod, and then pulled Frankie's razor sharp pawn shop sword from the sheathe and leapt over the wall.

Pain is a funny thing. It can drag you down and completely incapacitate you if you let it. Or, you can almost completely ignore it if you put your mind to it hard enough. Of course, it comes with the cost of potential further injury, but you *can* ignore it.

When I hit the ground on the other side of the wall, I expected a debilitating, lightning strike eruption of pain from my tailbone- or coccyx, as Larry would have called it- and I was prepared to endure and grind it out. As it happened, I didn't feel much of anything at all. I would love to say that it was the rush of adrenaline flooding my system that buffered me against the effects, but I'd learned too much to believe that.

As it was, I hit the ground running.

I wanted to savor the moment, to enjoy the soul lifting freedom of being allowed to do the job I loved, but I couldn't afford to. There was too much at stake for me to wallow in the luxury. Avery needed me.

The first thing I'd noticed after I'd thrown myself over the wall was the intense heat of the flames rolling against me as I landed just clear of their edge. The conflagration didn't touch me, but it was searing enough that my face felt scorched and I could feel blisters building on the ridges of my ears.

Wait, wait, wait, I thought sarcastically to myself. *You mean to tell me that fire is still hot?*

The back part of my mind giggled at my own wit, but the rest of me took a long second to take in my surroundings. Casting my gaze around, I realized that things were going better- or worse, depending on how you wanted to look at it- than I could have hoped.

The fire was doing exactly what I'd hoped it would do when I'd ordered the people of Branberry to light it: provide an effective barrier to the walls and burn down the "steps" of deaders that had fallen there earlier in the afternoon. I couldn't even begin to tell you how many others had walked into the blaze, moving mindlessly like moths toward a really big candle and adding human fuel. Whether they were physically impervious to pain or not, these stupid things didn't even have the sense to run away when they were on fire.

The bad side of it, though, was the sheer number of them. I hadn't given much concern when Frankie and I had gone out scavenging earlier. It had been alarming as we'd made our way back to Branberry from the grocery store. It had been daunting when Mackenzie and I had taken the dozers out beyond the walls. But now? There were simply too many to possibly attempt to count. I could only assume that both packs had finally converged, drawn by the light of our burning walls and the calls of their fellows.

Based on the number of deaders in my immediate vicinity, I should have been swarmed with in moments. Many of them, though, including some of the "smart" ones that had so far held themselves back, had started to converge further east, moving quickly to where Nancy and her Scottish terrier lay lifelessly in the dirt. In the wavering light of the flames, I saw three of them tear the dog apart, yanking on it savagely until the torso split. I didn't wait around to see what they did to Nancy. She was a hero for her sacrifice, and I wasn't about to waste the time that she had bought us. I searched out the shadowy outline of the Dakota in the darkness, finding it just as I heard the first sharp crack of Frankie's rifle. A smattering of other weapons discharging followed shortly thereafter.

I ran; I ran as hard and fast as I ever had. It would have been so convenient if the staggering, streaking deaders had provided me with a clear pathway as they had earlier, but right now that wasn't the case.

I weaved, I bounced, I jived; I slid through the harsh dirt of the desert floor, slipping my way around as many as I could as I made a beeline towards the truck. I only attacked when I had to, and while I would have felt more comfortable using the bat tucked into my belt, I went with the sword, if for no other reason than that it wasn't as loud.

Simple as it may seem, I didn't want the crunch of breaking bone to draw any attention my way.

When I did use Samantha, it was in quick sweeps and swipes that were only meant to throw the deaders off long enough for me to dash past. A cut to a hamstring here; a slice to an achilles tendon, there. Most took the debilitating wounds with a mindless sort of stoicism, turning their attention back to the burning bodies of their peers as I darted past.

I reached the Dakota much faster than I could have hoped. Heaving heavy breaths, I reached for the door handle. The molded black plastic handle lifted in my hand, but the door didn't open. The doors were locked. In the space of a single thought, I blessed Avery for her foresight, and cursed her for the inconvenience.

"Avery," I whispered urgently in a voice I doubted carried through the closed window. I tapped at the glass frantically with my free hand, hoping that she was still there to hear me. "Open up, c'mon, open up. It's me, c'mon."

It might well have been the longest few seconds of my life. I kept shooting furtive glances over my shoulder at the deaders that were streaming to where Nancy was, tapping urgently at the window the whole while. I was flooded with relief when Avery's tear streaked, snot nosed face peeked up at me. I heaved an inward sigh of relief; I'd made it in time. The sacrifices had been worth it.

I gestured animatedly, yanking at the handle, imploring her to unlock the vehicle. It was more than a little irritating when she shook her flushed face in a resounding "no," and unleashed a new gale of silent sobs as she pushed away from the window, climbing as far into the driver's seat as she could go.

God dammit, we don't have time for this.

Now, I'd always thought that it looked cool in the movies, but would be bullshit in reality. There was no way anyone could do *that*. I was on the precipice of decision, however, and was faced with two facts:

1. Avery wouldn't open the door.
2. Larry had told me that my body would go numb.

The pharmacist had never lied to me before, so I trusted his judgement. Suffice to say, it hurt like a mother fucker when I punched my fist through the window of the passenger side door.

Maybe I'd gotten overconfident in the almost forgotten pain of my broken tailbone, but dammit, I hadn't expected *this*. I felt something in my hand pop and splinter, and the skin of my knuckles split open from fine shards of glass. My entire hand felt like it had just been fed through a meat grinder, but I fumbled around on the inside of the window pane until I managed to pull the bolt lock up with a pop.

It was only after I'd withdrawn my arm and pulled the door open that I was forced to recall my words to Frankie earlier in the day: I have a bat; I could've just broken it. Part of me wanted to laugh uproariously, because, honestly, that's just funny. The bigger part of me just thought that my hand hurt. Seriously, no joke; it didn't feel good.

"We gotta go," I hissed between clenched teeth as Avery inched away from me, shaking her head. "*Now.*"

Nervous of cutting the girl on the naked blade, I tucked Samantha into my belt. Instinctively, I reached out with my broken and bleeding hand with the intention of grabbing her by the ankle and dragging her with me. I realized immediately, however, that my swelling fingers wouldn't have the strength to haul her out. Instead, I popped the bat out from my belt and transferred it to my bad hand. It was an unpleasant sensation to curl the fingers of my broken hand around the haft, but there was a familiar comfort, too.

I reached in with my good hand, grabbing Avery by the pant leg and pulling her towards me from across the center console. She squealed, but I didn't have any time to spare for gentle words or consolations. This wasn't the time to tell her that everything would be all right. I gave a final heave, and she slid out of the vehicle on her back. She would have fallen, crumpling in a heap to the dirt of the desert floor, but between the seat beneath her back and my own body standing in front of her she managed to stay upright.

I grabbed her roughly at the scruff over neck, tilting her chin so that her terrified eyes were forced to look into mine. I could feel her shaking in my hand, sad shudders that I could feel quaking through her entire body as fresh tears welled over the lids of her eyes. There was no way for me to tell if she was afraid of her predicament, or of me. I guess it really didn't matter, and I'd never been very good at that type of thing, anyway. I felt bad, though …

There was no time to delve into the discovery of the notion. Desperate as it was, my mad dash out to the Dakota had held its own type of enjoyment. Now, though, it was time for the hard part: getting back. Not hard on myself, mind you; I personally didn't really give a shit about what happened to me. But Avery wouldn't make it back on her own. It was my job to get her there. There was no time to explain things to her in detail, so I had to keep it simple.

"Stay by me. Do exactly what I say or you'll die."

Avery's eyes widened in new found terror, and I realized that I probably should have clarified my statement. I'm willing to concede that it was pretty open to interpretation on just exactly *who* would kill her: them, or me. I opted not to give her a chance to balk or respond. The fingers of my good hand were still wrapped around the nape of her neck, and after checking over both of my shoulders to make sure that our area was still clear I pushed away from the truck, dragging her beside me.

Guns and rifles were barking off to the east of our location in intermittent spurts, and the deaders continued to ignore us for the moment as they focused on the bait trifecta that I'd set up for them: visual light from the flames around the walls, sound from the cracking gun barrels, and the wonderful allure of fresh meat that wouldn't attempt to fight back. Between you and me, I felt a brief flash of shame. I really did feel bad about Chartreuse; that poor dog deserved better than what fate had given it.

I ran forward, dragging the reluctant Avery with me. She slipped and stumbled, her gangly, gawky, pre pubescent legs fumbling beneath her. My grip was the only thing that kept her moving forward. We made it almost twenty yards before one of the deaders noticed us. It was a female in the ragged remains of a teddy nightgown. The stained and tattered hem dangled just low enough to cover the undoubtedly rotten remains of her lady parts, but when she turned her milky eyes on us I had to resist the urge to gulp nervously. She wasn't a drone, or any random pack member; this was one of the thinkers.

I'm a bit ashamed to say that I froze up a bit in that moment, my momentum coming to a staggering halt as Avery gasped deep, frantic breaths at my hip. The female deader cocked her head at us like a curious sparrow before opening up the dark, rancid cavern of her mouth to bark. The gaunt mouth was filled with brown gums, and only a few remaining teeth that had turned black. Her lips pursed to call out to the rest of her pack.

"Broo-" she began, cutting off sharply as my silver bat took her across the jaw. Shriveled flesh split, dehydrated bone crunched, and her few remaining teeth flew from her mouth like a light hail storm. The damage had already been done, though. Abbreviated as it was, the first part of her call rebounded across the empty dome of the night sky. The movement of the deaders in our immediate vicinity slowed as they heeded the sound, creaking their unseeing eyes our direction and scenting the air in wet slurps. The gunfire from Nancy's wall went silent for a moment, only to be taken up with renewed intensity.

God dammit I love you, Frankie, I thought gratefully as his rifle spoke up loudly over the rest in a sharp three round burst. Frankie was an amazing marksman, with a wealth of experience that he wouldn't talk about. He was trained to make cool, calculated shots, one at a time. That three round burst was something else. It was a damn cacophony of gunfire from the end of the street, all designed to grab the attention of the deaders that had noticed us. Vacant eyes that had started to zone in on us turned back the other direction.

Avery shrieked from beside me, cupping her mouth as the female I'd felled rose to her feet. The deader's lower jaw was hanging free from her skull on one side, suspended by a few strands of flesh as it swung back and forth like a rotting pendulum. Normally, a clean shot like that would have dropped a deader like a stone, no matter how big it was. But even with the new strength of the virus in me, my broken hand didn't have the power to swing the way I normally would have.

I switched the bat to my left hand, holding Avery tight to my right hip, and swung as hard as I could at the deader's ankle. The blow, weak as it was from my bad hand (or was it my good hand, now that my good hand was my bad hand?) landed with the sharp *ting* of aluminum cracking into bone. The female's leg buckled, and she fell to the side with a loud woofing sound. It should have been a call, but since half of her face had been ripped away, it just came out like a loud burp.

This suited me just fine.

I'll find you later, I thought to myself as I hauled Avery behind me, stepping out of the way of her reaching arms as we darted past. We'd just moved beyond her when I heard a crunch of feet in the sand behind us. I whirled, striking at a drone that had managed to close in on my back. Left hand or not, this time the blow landed exactly as it should have, right in the hollow of the temple, and the thing fell. No time for my natural elation, though. Before the desiccated body was fully prone on the ground, I felt a sharp pull at my waist, and then an abrupt loosening of the jeans around my hips.

I suppressed my panic at the unforeseen contact, and looked over to see Avery's tear streaked face looking strangely resolute. It took only a scant second to realize what had happened: as I'd turned my back, Avery had grabbed the hilt of Frankie's sword from my hip. The razor sharp blade had cut clean through the cheap leather of my belt, and was now held in her shaking hands. The little girl held the blade- which was almost as long as she was tall- as best she could, point tilted up towards the black sky.

There was no time for words or discussion. I made eye contact with the preteen, and she gave me a nod, the sword trembling only slightly. I cocked my head towards the burning wall of Branberry in a "let's go" gesture, and she nodded once more.

I moved with urgency, pushing the quickest pace that Avery could keep. To be honest, she didn't really do too much with Frankie's sword, but I was proud of her for trying. I had to grab her by the shoulder to hustle her along a couple of times, but she returned the favor by thrusting Samantha's tip into the ribcage of a deader to hold it still long enough for me to crack it across the back of the dome. My little stowaway didn't even scream out when the shmagma of brain matter splattered across her chest. Good girl; I'd make an Exterminator out of her yet.

I felt an odd sense of pride as I thought this, but my enthusiasm was cut short when I realized that I wouldn't have much time to teach her the trade. No matter how hard I fought, no matter how much I held the infection at bay, I was bound to be dead within the week no matter what happened.

Kind of a depressing thought.

My lips tightened in agitation, and I grabbed Avery roughly by the back of her armpit, ushering her further on. My head was swiveling this way and that, looking for threats, but we were so close to the wall I could feel it. I put down two more that came into our path, and Avery, brave girl, gave a hacking swipe of the sword at the hamstring of a male drone that was creeping up on my left. Her strike wasn't hard enough to cut all the way through, but she managed to trip it to the ground where I took care of the rest.

Shots of gunfire continued to resound through the night sky, but deaders were starting to close in all around us, drawn from the bush towards the sound. There were too many to count, and mindless or not, they were bound to get to us. We had to make our move now, or everything was lost. We had to reach that wall. I pulled Avery up next to me.

"Run," I hissed into her ear. "Now. *Go!*"

I feared a repeat of earlier. I waited for her to balk and bolt back to the truck, making this entire endeavor fruitless. But the girl did me proud. She didn't argue or hesitate; she just ran forward as fast as her spindly legs would carry her, the sword bobbing awkwardly in her hands.

I snarled, slipping forward to land a few clean kill shots on a couple of deaders that might have blocked her passage. Left hand or not, the bat was light in my fingers and flew just the way it was supposed to. It was only when Avery began to scream out in wordless confusion that I realized something was wrong. I suppressed a long suffering sigh, but when I turned to look at her I realized the utter flaw in my plan; the plan that had worked so perfectly.

Deaders had gathered around the entire length of the wall, catching alight by those that were already burning. Those flames were what Avery was screaming at now; flames that covered the entire perimeter of Branberry's wall. I may have been able to leap through them on my way out, but there was no place for us to climb back up that wasn't covered in fire. We couldn't get back over.

Shit, I thought, well beyond irritated at the sudden inconvenience.

I'd been so proud of myself, so happy with how my plan had worked out- despite the unforeseen casualties- but now I was faced with the one aspect of my plan that I hadn't taken into consideration. What was even worse was that there was no time to think or try to problem solve. My greatest assets were utterly useless right now as I drew up next to Avery, the sword wavering in her shaking hands. She was looking at me in panic, waiting for me to tell her what to do, and I didn't have an answer.

The greater majority of the deaders were still moving past us, following the sounds of gunfire and the promise of fresh meat, but there were still more than enough that had broken away from the group to be a problem. And by "a problem," I mean kill us.

Brief as it may have been, we'd been out here long enough that we'd attracted considerable attention. Scores of dead eyes turned our direction and began to amble our way, picking up speed as they focused on us. There was no place for us to turn. The wall was right in front of us, within arms reach, but the wreath of flame prevented us from getting over.

Something very much like panic fluttered in my chest. It was an odd sensation. After all, I don't panic, ever. I simply don't have the capacity for that depth of emotion. Yet, here I was, with Avery depending on me to keep my promise to keep her safe.

The flames were high, rising a couple of feet over the edge of our wall. The putrid stench of the burning deaders stung my nostrils. The ash and cinder was making my eyes water. My hand was broken from punching through glass in my foolish attempt at heroism. The pain in my knuckles hadn't quite yet caught up to the numbness of my tailbone. I mean, hell, it had been a whole three minutes since it had happened. Maybe my expectations had been a bit too high. But I had to get Avery over that wall, and there was only one way that I could see to do it.

After all, the shortest distance between two points is a straight line. The straight line to safety was just in front of us, on the other side of Branberry.

I'd already decided that I was going to do my best to hurl the girl over the wall. My high school algebra quickly deduced that if I wanted to accomplish this without burning her, I'd have to get her roughly twelve feet into the air. I estimated Avery's weight at about eighty-five pounds. It was a tall task, but with the strength of the infection in me- broken hand or not- I felt like I could make that happen. The problem was that it left the girl with a twelve foot fall with nothing to catch her except hard concrete and rock.

"Lewis!" I screamed out to my best friend, knowing it was pointless but trying anyway. "I need you!"

I knew that there was no way that he could get there in time, even assuming that he'd heard me. I knew it in my gut. It was nothing but a last ditch, desperate hope. I needed someone there to catch her, since I couldn't be there to do it myself. It still had to happen, though; it was the only way to ensure her survival for at least a little bit longer.

Her ankles might break, a cold, dispassionate part of my mind intoned. *Maybe her arms, depending on how she lands. But she'll be alive. At least for a little bit longer. Or should I just kill her now? Would that be a kindness? Put her out of her misery before she knows what misery is?*

"I'm here!" a thready voice called from the other side of the wall, and for just a moment, I thought that Lewis had somehow miraculously heard me. It was hard to hear over the crackling whisper of flames, the constant pop of gunfire, and the grunting and barking of the deaders that were all around us, but my ears perked up, straining to hear the faceless voice on the other side of the wall. It definitely wasn't Lewis. As a matter of fact, given the circumstances, that voice could only belong to one person, and it was possibly that last person (outside of Nancy, of course) that I would have expected to come to my aid.

Sister Tracy.

I had my reservations, but there was no time to consider them. I knew that the aging nun was tough. I also knew that- tough or not- at her age, she was also liable to be frail, in body if not in spirit. The momentum of Avery's plummeting body was liable to cause her physical damage, assuming Sister Tracy could catch her at all. Assuming I could even get her over the wall.

God dammit, I don't have time for this. Too much thinking, not enough doing.

"Trust me," I said, dropping my second bat to the ground as I pulled Avery over to me. Broken or not, I was going to need both hands for this. She squawked loudly with a mixture of surprise and indignation as I grabbed her by the ass of her pants with my bad hand- I'm sure I don't need to tell you, but yes, it hurt- and the back of her neck. Her arms flailed, and Samantha's edge dragged across my shin. If it wasn't for my jeans, it would surely have cut me. Caught off guard by my sudden movement, Avery's arm whipped out instinctually. She lost her grip on the hilt of the sword, and it flew off to fall into the flames at the base of the wall.

When it rains, it pours. As if I didn't have enough to worry about, Frankie was going to be pissed that I lost his sword.

Deaders were closing in around us at an alarming rate as I clutched Avery in my hands like a side of beef. She hung at my waist, parallel to the ground, before I hoisted her up to chin level like an Olympic power lifter. Ignoring her sudden squawk, my muscles bunched and coiled as I gathered every ounce of strength in me.

I love you. I'm sorry, I thought as I heaved with every bit of power I had, tossing the girl through the air. She screamed as she left my hands, twisting and turning through the black night, flailing like a cat that had been dropped from a roof as she tried to right herself mid fall.

She cleared the flames. I watched her hit the apex of the toss and then begin the descent over the other side of the wall. Fast as it may have happened, Avery still managed to pull in another breath to shriek as she rolled over in mid air, the shrill call cutting through the night more effectively than even the gunshots did. I wanted to stay and watch, to hear Sister Tracy's affirmative response that she had successfully caught her, but in that moment- surrounded by deaders that had turned their full attention on me- I found that my instinct to keep living won out. I knew I had a deadline coming, but my survival instinct didn't want that deadline to be now.

Turns out that being *samurai* wasn't quite as glamorous as I'd anticipated. Fortunately for me, I didn't have any time to dwell on my cowardice. More than a dozen individual deaders had zoomed in on me, and I had to move, *now.*

I dodged to the side as the nearest lunged at me, casting a longing glance at my bat lying in the sand, beyond my reach. The male deader was small, with the spindly arms of a teenager on meth, and it didn't take much effort to shove him to the side and break his trajectory. The downside of the maneuver was that the force of my shove also propelled me back wards directly into the wall of flame climbing up the side of Branberry's perimeter.

Physics; what a bitch.

The feel of the heat was shocking and instantaneous. Flannel and denim may have been an effective barrier against deaders, but it wasn't nearly as well suited against flame. My contact with it was brief but undeniable. I rebounded instinctually, but was still there long enough that the left sleeve of my shirt caught fire. I couldn't help the natural scream that ripped it's way out of my throat. I may have always struggled with understanding or displaying emotion, but fear of fire is something that is ingrained in the DNA of every living being.

I slapped wildly at the flames licking against my skin as I continued to run forward, feeling fresh blisters growing against my skin. While the desert sand beneath my feet might have been a more effective means of smothering the flames, the concept of "stop, drop, and roll" didn't seem particularly wise for this scenario. To tell you the truth, Late Night Buyer, I didn't know what to do. My options were limited, so I did the only thing I could.

I ran away.

I had to run, you understand that, right?

Part of me wanted nothing more than to know that Avery was safe, but once she'd gone over the other side of the wall the situation had been taken out of my hands. I was no longer in control, and I kept telling myself that she wasn't my responsibility anymore. I'd done everything I possibly could, and I'd gotten her home. The best thing that I could do now, for everyone, was flee.

Right?

I don't know where I was running to; I just had to keep moving. I think most people would have had an natural inclination to stay close to the brightness of the flames, but as rational as the concept was it didn't seem like a smart move to me. I reasoned that, despite the affinity that people have to stay in the safety of a lit space, this was where the deaders were most likely to congregate. That had been the point of the fire, after all; to draw them in. So I did the thing that nobody was supposed to do, the thing that I'd directed my people to never, ever, do.

I slipped out into the darkness, delving into the unlit blackness of the desert where the deaders would hopefully be as blind as I was. I kept the bright lights of the burning walls on my left as a marker, and did my best to blend in with the shadows as I made my way west.

I was afraid. That might seem to be a stupid statement given the circumstances, but you have to understand that fear is an emotion that I'm not accustomed to having. I mean, don't get me wrong; I know when I'm *supposed* to be afraid- times and situations when normal people are afraid- but it's an emotion that only rarely makes an appearance in my lizard brain (much like most emotions and sensations I'm supposed to have.) The "flight" option had always been strangely absent in my fight or flight mechanism.

But now I felt true fear, and it was a truly unpleasant sensation that left a sour taste in my mouth.

It took every ounce of fortitude I had to regulate my breathing in a low, even pattern as I huddled inside of a thorny picker bush. Remaining as still as I could in the shadowed alcove, I resisted the urge to scratch at the sharp thorns that were digging into my skin, remaining motionless as I watched a large group of deaders stalk past me. I couldn't make out individual features. Their bodies were like a deeper, darker shade of night.

They were barely past me before I scrambled out of the meager safety of the thorny branches. I cast my eyes over to my left, where the light from the flames cast out its ambient glow, illuminating the area. Part of me- a big part, actually- wanted nothing more than to throw myself into the fray, to go hand to hand with the animals surrounding me until I was ripped apart. Even weaponless, I figured I could take down five, maybe six, before the end came. The better, wiser, part of me just wanted to make it home. It was in that moment that an idea occurred to me. It was a simple idea, one that probably should have occurred to me sooner, but better late than never. I ran a few quick, simple facts through my head.

1.   Half of the perimeter of Branberry was still burning intensely. The logical step, then, was to find an area that wasn't on fire. This, in turn, lead to the next issue:

2.   The walls were high enough that I wouldn't be able to scramble over them. As best as I could tell, our front gate was the closest section of wall that wasn't burning, but it was also the highest point of our perimeter. I wouldn't be able to get my hands over the edge without someone to help me up or something to stand on. I couldn't use the crumpled bodies of the deaders the same way that I had earlier in this longest of days, so I needed something else to use as a stepping stone.

Ahh … Light bulb.

This was my "ah-hah" moment, and it sent my mind spiraling towards the next portion of what would be my solution.

3.   Martin had said it himself earlier in the day when Mackenzie and I had taken the dozers out: "She wasn't stupid enough to let the truck run out of gas," he'd said. "Went down our street, pulled up next to the wall, and hopped out." Bingo.

If I could make it to the opposite side of Branberry, I could use the Chevy as a step to get over the wall; to get back to my people for as long as I could. It was a long shot, filled with risk, but it might just work. All I had to do now was make it over to Rocky Coast, the street that sat on the other side of Branberry.

Weaponless. Surrounded by hundreds of deaders. At night.

And here I thought I wouldn't get my rush, today. I bit my lip with a surge of eagerness at the new challenge, and took off in a silent, loping sprint. I almost didn't even notice that I'd bitten hard enough to draw blood.

Almost.

It was only a football field of distance to make it to the gate, but it was a *long* football field, if you know what I mean. My timing had to be almost perfect when I made my dash, but I realized that I was also relying heavily on blind luck as much as anything else. The flames from the wall were still burning strong, and the light breeze in the air continued to pervade my nostrils with the hideous stench of the burning deaders.

The concussive sound of gunfire still reached my ears, but the time between shots had grown longer. I don't know if it was because my people were trying to conserve ammo, or if it was because the Thinkers were all that were left, and that they'd decided to return to the tactic of holding back out of harm's way. Either one was a losing option for the people of Branberry. The deaders either gathered in numbers, waiting for the flames to die down before they attacked and swarmed the walls … or my family and friends eventually ran out of bullets, and *then* the deaders attacked and swarmed the walls. Neither one was a winning scenario for the people of Branberry.

I moved in a low crouch, ducking and running when I saw openings. I was well beyond the cleared ring of desert that encircled Branberry, tiptoeing as quickly as I could around and in between the desert growth and debris. I pressed myself back into the painful bite of pricker bushes more than once, dropped down to lie prone in a gully, and literally stood perfectly still while holding my breath on several occasions as small groups and packs of deaders moved around me.

The shadows were my friend, but like I said, I was relying on blind luck as much as anything else. Yet, I wondered if that fickle lady had an eye for me in that moment. I slipped, moved, and dodged, standing still when I had to, and none of them noticed me. The hardest part of it was how strong the driving instinct to attack them was becoming. It almost felt like my need compelling me, but somehow wasn't quite right.

I'd lived with my urges my entire life, and I knew the ebb and flow of them to the very core. This wanton recklessness in me was something else, and before I made my next quick dash to the last stand of desert shrub before reaching our gate, I cast a quick look at my left wrist. There was just enough ambient light from the flames for me to hold my arm out past the shadowed barrier of the desert tree I was currently hiding in. I twisted my arm around slowly, so as not to draw attention from any milky eyes that might have been turned my way.

The half moon ring of teeth marks on my wrist were puffy and inflamed, protruding up from the skin like a snake bite or fresh tattoo. I could see faint shadows of my veins crawling up my forearm. Maybe it was a trick of the light, but they looked like thin, black tendrils of tree root slithering up my arm. I swiped a finger across my forehead, and despite the cool night air, a thick sheet of sweat sluiced from my brow.

I slipped my arm back in, and then looked right and left. A trio had just passed me, barking and coughing, but all I saw was their backs. The rest of the area was clear for a moment, and I could feel Lady Luck winking at me. This was liable to be my best chance. I slithered between the sharp brambles of thorns as quietly as I could, and once I'd seen that the space was clear, I sprinted as hard as I could push myself. I expected to feel sluggish, but instead I blurred across the uneven terrain.

It was an odd sensation to be moving that fast. It might not have been the singular fastest sprint of my life, but given that both my hand and tailbone were undoubtedly broken- and, quite frankly, that I'd had a particularly long day- it was surprising. I noted distantly that my butt didn't hurt at all, my hand felt manageable, and even the fresh burns on my arm were only mildly annoying. Hell, I wasn't even breathing hard from the exertion. The only thing that really stood out to me- and it was demanding my attention more and more by the second- was that I was extremely thirsty. Seriously, like, throat hacking thirsty. My throat and tongue felt like eighty grain sandpaper.

I was at our gate before I knew it, huddling down on my haunches with my back against a pile of tires that we'd stacked near the entrance. I felt like I'd been dragged through the longest three hours of my life, even though I knew it couldn't have been more than ten minutes since I'd thrown Avery over the wall. Still, it had been a long ten minutes.

I held my position, the small of my back pressed against the hard rubber of the stacked tires as I panted in air. It was more from my adrenaline dump than the sprint, but I once again forced myself to regulate my breathing. It was harder to do than it normally was.

Crouched down on my haunches, back pressed against the tires, I took a brief moment to take in my surroundings. There were groups of deaders straggling, prowling, and stalking in the distance, but there were none near me at this moment. Keeping my back pressed against the wall, my eyes darting constantly for a threat, I worked my way down the length of the cinder block wall until I reached Rocky Coast.

Their gate looked much like ours, but it was smaller, flimsier, and had been broken open. The hinges that had held it secure had been torn from the cinder block walls, leaving a wide breach. I slipped through the opening, my back hugging the wall, and even in the darkness of night I could see the carnage. Shadowed forms lay like splayed humps in the middle of the street. It was impossible to tell if they were deader or human, and in the lightless night, I guess it didn't really matter. Dead was dead.

Doors and windows were shattered in jagged edges, like the mouth of a psycho ward patient with filed teeth. At the end of the street I saw a construction that had crumbled like a broken spider and I realized that it was a gazebo that had been erected for the wedding that they'd been hoping to celebrate. The tattered remains of streamers fluttered along the ground despondently, like the broken dreams of a dying child.

There were two other things I noticed within the first few seconds on the street: the Chevy that Mackenzie had been driving, parked haphazardly near the blank wall that separated our two streets, and the three dozen or so deaders meandering between me and the truck. None had noticed me, but I would have a hard time getting through them unscathed. I glanced around, looking for something, anything, that I could use as an effective weapon. That's when I saw it. It wasn't my bat, but I felt like it could get the job done: a loose length of chain that had fallen free when the gate had been ripped open.

I crept over, hunched down and with my eyes always on the deaders, and wrapped my hand through the links, coiling it around my wrist. Despite everything that had happened in the last twelve hours, despite the urgency of the impending threat to Branberry or my own descending death, I couldn't deny the urge of excitement that flowed through me as the chain links clinked together lightly. While it probably would have been indiscernible at any other time, in the relative silence of night it seemed loud. I saw several sets of gleaming dead eyes swivel my way, their bodies outlined by the pervading glow of our burning walls. I could hear Frankie's voice singing in the back of my head like a low thrum.

As much as I wanted to I didn't attack them; I had to be disciplined. My only goal and focus was to make it over the wall, and the odds weren't in my favor if I tried to take them all on. Still, blood had to be spilled if I was going to make it there, and I found myself humming under my breath as I moved forward.

The opening salvo to "Welcome to the Jungle" purred softly in my throat as I began to drip the length of the chain on the ground like a fisherman's bobber. The steel links created a clinking sound that reminded me of Christmas. More eyes looked my way as I slowly walked around the perimeter of Rocky Coast's broken walls.

That's it, I thought in grim satisfaction as they all started to zone in on me. *I've got your fun and games right here.* They probably couldn't see me, but they were attracted by the sound. They drew together with an eerie sort of grace, converging like a flock of birds, with a single male taking point. He was an ugly son of a bitch, but his shambling posture took on a decidedly aggressive focus as he stalked me. I had become his center of interest. The pack had opted to follow him, which meant I'd become the pack's center of interest.

This suited me just fine. They may not have been able to see me clearly, but they'd picked up on the sound and were growing more agitated by the moment. I knew it was just a matter of moments before their blood lust took them and they attempted to blitz me.

"Learn to live like an animal in the jungle where we play," I said under my breath.

Fuck this, I thought with a savage snarl, my patience and restraint evaporating like rain in a Vegas summer as I surged forward into the closely quartered pack, whipping the heavy length of chain back and forth as viciously as I could with my left hand.

Like I said, patience has never been one of my virtues.

Outside of cinema, I don't think anyone in their right mind has ever considered what it would be like to hit someone in the face with a heavy gauge chain, but the damage was more than I could have hoped for. The weight of my blows had enough force to knock the deaders to the side, but even in the dim light I could see the links tearing through any of the rotten flesh they connected with, ripping it off in ragged strips. The stupid things were still streaking towards me with ungainly grace, but my sudden attack had thrown off the balance of their attack. A distant part of me was halfway amused to realize that I was still singing Frankie's song. *Yeah, you can take any ol' thing you want,* I thought …

"But you ain't gonna take it from me," I hissed out loud, my voice a whisper slithering between my lips but gaining strength as my need took over.

I lost myself in the lyrics. The recesses of my mind provided the aggressive background music: the sawing guitars, the thumping bass, the clanging drums and hi-hats. I fell into a rhythm at the staccato beat, and my length of chain followed suit as it whipped back and forth as quickly as I could lash it. To my eye, the end of the chain seemed to be moving slowly, like a helicopter revving up, but when it made contact, the deaders were knocked to the side. They didn't always fall, but they staggered like knock kneed drunkards stumbling out of a bar.

Centrifugal force, I thought, dredging up old terminology from my college physics class. I lashed out with the chain once more, cracking it straight forward from my hip like a bull whip. A deader collapsed like a pinata that had had its string cut, and I smiled to myself. I've always liked physics.

"If you want it you're gonna bleed, but that's the price you pay!"

A dim part of my mind recognized that I was screaming, but I didn't care. I slung the rippling chain in heavy sweeps. The length of connecting links would buckle and collapse when I connected with a deader, but the bright side was that the deader would buckle and collapse, too- Score!- and I'd whip it back for another attack.

"In the jungle, welcome to the jungle!"

One managed to grab me by the right arm, biting deep into the sleeve of my flannel. The power of its jaws clamping together on my already wounded limb was excrutiating. Its teeth ground back and forth, bruising my flesh, but the flannel did its job, holding strong and stopping the teeth from sinking into my skin. Call me selfish, but- infected and dying or not- I had no inclination to being eaten while I was still drawing breath. Seriously; at least buy me a drink, first.

I drove the knuckles of my left hand into the side of its skull. I must have hit a soft spot, because I heard the crunch of breaking bone beneath my hand as it fell to the side, releasing its mouth hug on my other arm.

I recovered, and the chain kept swinging. The Chevy was only a few more walking bodies away.

Shouting in wordless fury/ ecstasy, I whipped the chain low at the ankle of my nearest target. The links wrapped around the desiccated calf, and I gave a hard yank, snapping its feet out from under it. The deader landed on its back with a thump, floundering to regain its feet. Watching it hit the ground drove my need with a feverish frenzy. I shrieked out, my voice hitting a pitch that was maniacal to my own ears; Axl Rose would have been proud.

"You're gonna!-"

"Die" should have been the final word, but I cut off at the last second. I was focused on killing, doing the only thing I'd ever been good at, but in that moment I saw a clear path towards the Chevy. There was only one deader left in my immediate range, and I could already tell that it wasn't going to be a problem. The bastard was streaking at me from my right, snarling and slavering, but both of its arms had been ripped off at the elbow. I didn't even consider it a threat.

I wanted to finish Frankie's song; truly, I did. I was in the zone, and- if I'm being honest- it was a really good song. But in that split second, cold reality reasserted itself, and this wasn't the time for singing. If I could get this last deader out of the way, I had a clean line towards the Chevy. So I did what any rational person would do: I changed my level, dropping my shoulder, and barreled into it like a defensive linebacker with a clear shot at the quarterback.

I hit it right at the hip- the sweet spot- and the creature buckled like a book that had been slammed closed. The filthy soles of its shoed feet left the ground as it flew backwards to land in a squirming heap. It fluttered around, but without hands it couldn't stand back up. That quickly, my path to the Chevy was clear, and I wasn't going to waste the opportunity.

I was panting heavily from exertion, but I ran forward as fast as my driving legs could propel me. I let the length of chain slither from my wrist to the ground as I vaulted myself over the edge and into the bed of the pick up. My feet landed with a creaking thud that was loud in the dark night, and I heard the barking call of dozens of other deaders spring up at the sound of the impact.

Didn't matter to me, though; they were all too far away to be a threat, and the lip of the wall to Branberry was practically within reach. I bounded up onto the roof of the cab, causing a couple more loud thumps of buckling metal, and then leapt out at the wall. My fingers caught the edge of concrete, sending a muted scream through my bad hand, and the skin of my palms scraped painfully as I scrambled. My feet fluttered for purchase against the sheer surface, but my grip held. I slung leg up over the ledge, and then -carefully, this time- dropped myself down over the other side.

I was home.

Somehow, against every ridiculous odd stacked against me, I'd made it home. I managed a few staggering steps, heaving in frantic breaths, before all of my adrenaline went out of me. It had been the strength that had kept me going, but when it dumped out, my body went with it. The strength left my limbs, and I felt an odd tingling in my fingers and toes. My vision waivered, turning hazy, and I suddenly found it hard to keep myself upright. My head felt heavy, and I considered it a minor victory that I managed to fumble my panic whistle out of my pocket. I didn't get it to my mouth on the first try, and when I did manage it, I was only able to emit a short, piercing warble before I passed out and tumble to the ground.

My last thought before my eyes finally closed was about how thirsty I was.

The darkness whispered at me. I didn't recognize it, but I felt like I should have. Something about it seemed familiar, sounded familiar. Wrapped in the velvety blackness of this endless abyss, I couldn't quite grasp it.

"Cleet," a voice whispered at me, the twanging tone worming its way through the darkest corners of my mind like the thinnest of serpents. I wanted to ignore it. I wanted to just sink back down into the black comforter of oblivion.

"Cleet," the voice rang again, this time with more urgency, and I felt the rhythmic tapping of a hand against my chin. The contact drew me out of the comforting darkness, and the closer I got to the surface, the more acutely I felt the sting of the callused palm swatting against my cheek. My vision was blurry as my eyelids finally fluttered open to reveal the hazy lines of the face above me. The image blurred into two wobbly twins, but gradually coalesced into Frankie's plump face looking down on me with concern. He was still wearing his FSU hat, but it had been darkened and dampened through out with sweat.

"Ungh," I grunted, drawing in a pained breath. Fresh air sluiced down my gullet, and my throat and mouth felt like a stairway lined with razor blades.

"Get up, bitch," my brother in law said, his voice halfway lifeless with forced humor as he pulled me by the arm into a sitting position. My mind was swimming through a fog. I vaguely felt my arm go around his shoulder, felt my ass lift from the ground, felt Frankie halt as he struggled to pull my weight up …

Strong as he was, Frankie was struggling with my dead weight. It was only when I felt another body press itself against my other armpit, hoisting me upright, that I regained any sense of lucidity. My vision was still fighting against me, refusing to focus, but I tilted my chin to my left to see a hazy shadow of pure blackness. Something in my lizard brain lashed out, associating the dark form that I couldn't see with swarms of deaders trying to kill me. I started to thrash around, my limbs flailing weakly, and it was only as my swooning vision cleared that I recognized the diminutive figure helping to support me.

Sister Tracy, decked out in her full black gown and habit. The fabric of her smock looked rumpled, like it had been rolled up and tucked away for a long time, but was still as spotless and clean as anything I'd seen her wear. The old nun caught the dumbstruck look on my face, shrugging my arm further over her shoulder.

"There are times when the Lord is needed," she huffed as she held me up, turning her steely, resolute gaze forward. "This seems to be one such. It's my sacred duty to be here in his absence."

"Avery," I croaked. Speaking felt like it was harder than it should have been. Even aside from the wounds I'd taken- wounds that I couldn't even feel, anymore- my skin felt taut, like dried parchment that had been stretched too far. My skin felt like a full bodied jacket. My jeans felt loose around my hips, and for some reason I was acutely aware of my ribs pressing against my skin.

"The girl is safe," Sister Tracy said. "Scared, but safe. My shoulders and knees hate you more than my heart ever did, but you brought her safely back to us. You brought her home."

The old nun didn't say anything else, but she really didn't need to. She wouldn't look at me, and I could see that she was struggling beneath my weight, but there was something in her posture and blank stare. In her own way- whether she liked me or not- Sister Tracy was conveying her gratitude.

Part of me crumbled in that moment. Walls that I hadn't known I'd erected tumbled to the ground, and I allowed myself to release a pent up breath I hadn't known I'd been holding.

Avery was safe. If I did nothing else worthwhile in my life, I could rest assured that, in this moment, I was in fact a good person.

"Where's Lewis?" I asked, my dried voice barely more than the sound of glass shards grinding together. It came out as little more than a whisper, but I didn't miss the way that Frankie's already blank face hardened. His normally bluff features had been flat, but now they took on a lifeless tone.

"Have this," a voice said, distracting me, and I recognized Larry's voice as he strode forward. Forestalling anything that Frankie might have said, the pharmacist held a crinkled bottle of water out to me. The label was peeling, and I knew that the water was nothing more than what we'd been able to scavage. My reclusive house-mate looked rumpled and weary, but there was a certain, quiet, intensity to him at the moment. I almost didn't even notice it; I was focused on his offering.

My eyes locked onto it with a mechanical intensity that I could almost feel, and I pulled my arm from Sister Tracy's shoulder to grasp the rumpled bottle. The thin plastic compressed in my hand, sloshing water out over the top, and I slammed it hard to my lips. I swallowed again, and again, chugging the tepid fluid until the tiny container was empty.

I heaved in a jagged breath that had a little more of my normal voice to it. The water felt like a lead weight in my stomach, but it was also strangely invigorating, too. I could practically feel energy flowing back into me, and the constricting tightness of my skin seemed to loosen up a bit. I moved to hand the empty bottle back to Larry, but was surprised to see that he had disappeared, melting back into the shadows that cloaked Branberry.

"Where's Lew?" I asked again, sounding almost like myself. I'd regained my equilibrium, and managed to hold myself up, slipping my arm from around Frankie's shoulder. My brother in law still didn't answer, and I took a closer look at his face; his dark, unreadable face. His expression- or lack there of- made my blood run cold.

Frankie wasn't right.

I felt my heartbeat speeding up once more, but this time it wasn't about adrenaline or exertion. There was an unpleasant sensation building in my gut, a cold feeling, and I didn't like it. Frankie's face remained utterly unreadable and impassive. He wouldn't look at me, his gaze pointed straight towards the other side of the street.

"He ain't here, right now," he said after a drawn out moment, voice tight and terse. He was still pointedly not looking at me.

"What do you mean?" I asked, an edge to my voice, wishing I had more water. "Get him the fuck out here; we need to go over everything. It's bad out there."

Frankie didn't answer, and I was surprised when Sister Tracy spoke up.

"Lewis is no longer with us," the old nun said. Her voice was firm and stalwart, but it had the forced strength of a funeral director speaking to a grieving family. "His resolve waivered. He lost his faith, and committed the most cardinal of sins. He has refused salvation."

My heart skipped a beat as my stomach plunged, refuting the implications. *Wait,* I thought, dumbstruck, *what do you mean?*

"Lew's dead," Frankie said into the silence, answering my unspoken question as he spit off to the side.

The words reached my ears, but didn't make it all the way to my brain. My heart began to pound in my chest, and it had nothing to do with my recent activities, or the poison pulsing in my system. My heels stopped in their tracks, and I felt like an invisible, daunting weight had settled over me, forcing me down.

"Jamie-Lynn killed herself," Frankie said, flatly, his voice as featureless as his expression.

That's it! A part of me thought, and I had to resist the urge to snap my fingers together in satisfaction. *Jamie-Lynn!* The bigger part of me just wanted to refuse what I was hearing.

"She was taking care of Nancy," Frank continued, his mouth twisted in distaste, like he'd bitten into something foul. He still wouldn't make eye contact with me, his flat stare turned instead towards the burning walls that shrouded us. "Lew found'er. He went there to check on them after you went over the wall, and get them to the pool." He paused before continuing. "He ate a bullet."

Maybe it was my overwrought mind not working as fast as it normally did, but it took me a moment to register precisely what Frankie was saying, and then to translate it to myself. *"Jamie-lynn is dead; Lew ate a bullet,"* became *"Lewis found his lesbian girlfriend- the girl he's loved since high school- dead in a bathtub. After that, he put the barrel of his gun inside his mouth and pulled the trigger."* The flat, blank expression of Frankie's face was the only confirmation I needed.

My best friend- my only friend- was dead.

"The guilt of her urges must have been too much for her to bear," Sister Nancy continued, unaware of my lack of interest in her preaching. A detached portion of my mind was registering her words from far, far, away. The nun's unintentional revelation that I hadn't been the only one on Branberry that knew the woman's secret was lost on me.

God dammit, Lew.

"I've been working with her, trying to steer her back to the path of righteousness, but the child's guilt and perversion were too much for her to carry."

You stupid son of a bitch; what did you do?

"The gift of life is a blessing from the Lord. To throw his gift away is the acceptance of eternal damnation."

I knew that girl would be the death of you.

"We've lost two souls this evening."

I won't lie to you, Late Night Buyer; part of my world collapsed in that moment. Over the entirety of my life, there weren't too many people that I could say I cared about; like, truly *cared* about. Oh sure, the people of Branberry were important to me, but that's because I was their Exterminator. They were my responsibility, and they gave me a purpose. But truly *care* about? I could've counted them all off on one hand with enough fingers left over to flip you the bird.

Lewis had quite possibly been the most important of them all. He'd been a sibling to me in a way that Frankie, or even Lacy, never could have been. He and I had been equal and opposite; Yin and yang. Now- and I could only blame it on his foolish attachment to a woman that would never love him the way he loved her- I was Yangless, and it had happened in the blink of an eye. I hadn't even been there to talk to him, to help him see sense.

Our fifteen year friendship flashed through my mind at warp speed: cackling laughter, insane stunts, the dares of childhood. Him standing at my shoulder at my parents wake, while Lacy cried against my hip. Holidays, birthdays, weekends; fights, scraps, arguments and debates.

The good,the bad, the ugly. The way that we'd worked together to build Branberry, when everyone else around us seemed to be dying as the world crumbled. It was all done.

I felt like I should have been feeling something more than the numb detachment I was experiencing. I owed him that. Instead, I was as tearless as the day they'd lowered my parents into the ground.

"You should also know," Frankie spoke up, breaking my thoughts and Sister Tracy's gospel, "that ol' Nancy is missin', too."

Frankie turned to look at me for the first time since he'd helped me from the ground. His face and eyes were still flat and blank, utterly devoid of emotion. The movement caught my attention, drawing me out of my reverie. It was an expression I'd only seen on Frankie's face a handful of times, and he only adopted it when there was killing to be done.

"Strange thing, that," he continued. "Can't imagine where that ol' girl would've run off too."

I can, I thought, *and since I sent you down to her area of the wall, I'm guessing that you do, too. Did you see her, Frankie? Did you catch a glimpse beneath the pushing, grasping bodies of the deaders piling atop her, tearing her apart? Did you catch sight of her- an arm that had been ripped loose, maybe- through the scope of your rifle?*

I returned Frankie's bland stare and flat expression. Each of us was waiting for the other to give something away. A second or two of heavy silence ticked by.

"It's a pity 'bout Chartreuse," Frankie finally said, breaking the silence. Sister Tracy had finally shut her mouth, looking on in rigid confusion. The nun might have been in the dark, but Frankie had just told me all I needed to know: he knew.

We stared at each other without blinking, holding an odd sort of speechless conversation as we both went through the mental calculations of trying to decipher what the other was thinking. My side of the wordless conversation went something like this:

He knows. How much does he know? Does he know about Jamie-Lynn? If he does, does he understand? Can he know that Larry helped me get the heroine to Nancy? I didn't even want that garbage here; it was your idea to keep it, Francis. Not my fault if I found a purpose for it. You gonna kill me, Frankie? I'm probably close to dead, anyway. Lew's dead; you can't hold me responsible for that. That was his decision. I was only doing what had to be done. My clock is ticking. I got Avery back, but we aren't in the clear, yet. Let me do what I can while I'm still able to do it.

Now, you'd have to ask Frankie himself, but I'd imagine that his thought process might have gone something like this:

What the fuck did you do, Cleet? Are you out of your Goddamn mind? How sick are you, right now? How deep has that bite gotten into you? I can't trust you, anymore. We had a deal, but I don't know if I can hold to it. I didn't like Nancy none, but hell, man, she didn't deserve none o' that. What the fuck am I supposed to do now, huh? What about Lacy? What the hell am I supposed to tell her? She ain't gonna understand. I gotta do what has to be done, and I lose either way.

I liked Frankie. Maybe even more than liked. In terms of *care*, he was one of the few people on my hand. More importantly, he made sure that my sister was taken care of. That mattered to me. Hillbilly or not, he protected her in a way that I never could.

Neither one of us could afford to kill the other just yet.

"Where's Avery?" I asked in a level voice as Frankie and I continued to stand eye to eye. The soft question hung in the night air, and finally provided Sister Tracy with a reason to speak up.

"The child is with your sister," the old nun said, her face tinted with a hint of confusion at the abrupt change of topic. Tracy may have been in the dark regarding the tension floating about us, but Frankie caught the nuance of what I was getting at. I could see it in his face, and it spoke to me like words written on a page. More so, I think he got the same impression from me.

I know what I did. I know that you know. It wasn't exactly the way that I wanted it to happen, but I saved the girl that you took as a daughter by doing so.

Frankie scratched at his nose with the back of his knuckles, and twisted the sweat stained brim of his Seminoles cap back and forth over his brow. Was it just this morning that he'd found that? God, it seemed like so much longer. His face was stained with soot, but he gave me a curt nod. I couldn't have told you exactly where his head was at, but I took that to mean our deal was still in tact for the moment. I nodded back to him. It was the most emotion I could summon up, but Frankie grasped it for what it was worth.

"Where do we stand?" I asked. Now that Avery was home- and call me selfish, but since I'd somehow managed to survive, as well- it was time to get back to business. I wiped my broken hand across my forehead, swiping away a stream of sweat from my brow. The falling drops of perspiration left dark stains on the ground, and while Sister Tracy didn't seem to take account of it, I didn't miss the way that Frankie's cool gaze nonchalantly followed the movement.

"Wall is standing strong," my brother in law said at the same moment that Sister Tracy- in a solemn voice suitable for a funeral parlor- said "Would you like to see Lewis?"

Did I want to see Lew? That was a hell of a question. *Ate a bullet,* Frankie had said. Did I want to see my best friend with the top of his head blown off? See what was left of him? Or maybe it was selfish of me to even look at it from that perspective. Lew had been the leader and organizer of Branberry; did I want to see him lying stiff and cold? I'd never been squeamish at the sight of blood, but the answer to either question was a resounding "no."

"Is he dead?" I asked. I wasn't looking at either of them, but the question was directed at Frankie. My brother in law sighed before answering.

"Yeah," he said, some of the tension seeping out of him at the admission. "He is."

"I'll take your word for it," I said. "Seeing him isn't going to change anything. Now let's take a look at the perimeter," I finished, walking forward once more.

I stood at the top most point of the roof, in the same spot that used to be Lewis's perch, and watched the burning walls of Branberry. A part of me almost felt like I could still sense his presence, here.

The flames continued to crackle and flicker, billowing great clouds of choking smoke into the air. The deaders had provided most of the fuel, but it was starting to run down. Not because we were running out of deaders, but because the greater mass of them had decided- or finally learned- to hold themselves back beyond our reach at the edge of our desert perimeter. Even in the darkness I could see the glowing green glints of countless eyes, and I worried how many of the smart ones had played a role in that. I'd ordered everyone to stop shooting. We could have continued, I guess, but what would have been the point? Even if every bullet fired flew true, I doubted we had enough ammo to put them all down.

For now, we had to rely on the flames. That meant keeping them going, and since the deaders had stopped providing the fuel, we needed something else. The citizens of Branberry were busy breaking apart furniture to toss over the walls. Much of it had been pulled from the vacant homes, but here and there people lugged some piece of their own out. Everything could have served a purpose, but our current situation meant that the only thing they were good for was burning.

Table legs, couch cushions, battered TV trays; They were all tossed over the wall into the flames, spurring them to fresh levels. The flames crackled enthusiastically, fueled by polyester, wood varnish and lacquer, and the twined yarn of floor carpets rolled up into thick tubes. The flames welled up anew with an almost ironic intensity. Why would I call it ironic, you ask? Well, I guess because we were all taking the things we loved and destroying them so that we could survive until tomorrow, and if tomorrow ever came, we would all be bleaker because those treasured things weren't there.

Me? I wasn't doing well, and I knew it. It wasn't just the loss of Lewis, or the guilt I should have felt over Nancy and Jamie-Lynn. No, those emotions had been locked away for another time that would probably never come. My concerns were of a far more basic nature. While standing atop Lew's old spot on the roof made me possibly the most visible citizen on the street, it also afforded its own sort of privacy. It allowed me my own space of solitude to breath, to think, and I used that time to evaluate myself.

The bite on my arm looked bad. The wound itself was simple enough, the type of thing that should have required nothing more than a bandage. But this wasn't a bite from your typical neighborhood mutt or toddler. The skin on my forearm was darkened and inflamed, the veins black and swollen against the skin like a heroin addict's hardened vessels. My right hand was swollen like a water balloon, purpling around the edges, but at least I couldn't feel the pain it should have been causing me. I couldn't even imagine what my ass and lower back must have looked like. I hadn't really had an opportunity to evaluate myself in a mirror, but fortunately I couldn't feel that, either.

Small blessings, people; take'em where you can get'em.

There was a decent burn along my arm from where I'd crashed into the outside wall. Blisters puckered against my skin, trailing down my forearm. If they'd gone any further, they may have just cauterized the half moon ring of teeth marks. I'd barely noticed them until now, but once I had, they refused to be ignored. I could feel a muted sort of pain singing to me. I'm no pro, but I'm familiar enough with burns to know that, if I could feel these, then they probably would have been excruciating under different circumstances. None of this was the worst part, though.

The worst part, the most concerning part, was my fever.

It didn't feel like a fever. I didn't have body aches, there was no chill, but I knew the symptoms well enough to recognize it as such.

My hands- which had never once in my life trembled- were shaking like a leaf in a strong breeze. Sweat was pouring down my temples like a rainfall, dripping into my face and eyes. I couldn't even shift my stance without a multitude of droplets falling around my feet. My face felt sunken and drawn, especially around my eyes. My skin felt like taut Ceran-wrap stretched across my face.

It was all an effect of the virus, and I knew it, but that didn't make it any easier to accept. I felt a heavy moment of self doubt. I'd promised Frankie that I could hold it at back, keep it at bay, but I was realizing that maybe I didn't have quite as much choice in the matter as I'd originally thought. I was pondering all of this when I collapsed. I'd been swooning, and hadn't even realized it, swaying side to side until I unbalanced myself.

The hard tiles cracking into my ribs- breaking my fall- jolted me back to awareness, and I scrambled at their smooth surface, scrambling frantically for a grip as the lower half of my legs slid over the edge of the house. I anticipated the impending fall, and was mildly surprised when I felt two hands press against the bottom of my thrashing foot. The pressure against my sole heaved, and while it didn't stop my plummet completely, it was enough of a resistance that I was able to slow my descent and scramble to maintain my precarious position.

"Easy, easy," a soft voice said from below me. "I've got you."

The support of the hands beneath my foot sagged, and while I wouldn't call my journey to the ground a gymnastic masterpiece, I could at least call it a controlled tumble or falling with grace. Against all odds, I managed to land on my feet, stumbling into the side of the house.

"You all right, Boss?" Larry asked from where he'd backed away to avoid my falling self.

"Yeah," I panted after a moment, pushing myself away from the wall to stand as straight as I could. God, I was thirsty.

As if he'd read my mind, Larry picked up a plastic gallon milk jug filled with water from where he'd set it. My mind registered what it was before my eyes had fully focused on it. Same as earlier, I couldn't tear my gaze away from it. I *needed* it. In that moment, if I had to choose between breathing and drinking that water … well, breathing is overrated, anyway.

"Here," Larry said, bobbing the jug in his hand suggestively. I didn't have to be told twice. The mouth of the repurposed milk jug was at my lips in an instant, and I chugged convulsively. I gulped as quickly as I could, taking mouthfuls so large that they made my esophagus stretch uncomfortably.

"It's dehydration," Larry said as I continued to inhale the water as fast as I could get it down my gullet. "Can you see that?"

I broke away from the jug, dragging in a sharp intake of breath. I guess my earlier conviction to not breath in lieu of the water wasn't as stalwart as I'd thought. Thick streams that had leaked from my lips dribbled down my chin. I looked at the jug in my hand, and saw that half of the contents were gone.

"What are you talking about?" I asked, swiping a clean spot on my sleeve across my mouth. I wasn't overly concerned about infection at this point.

"*Water,*" he said, placing emphasis on the word. It was hard to tell in the dark night, but our skittish pharmacist seemed particularly urgent. "I don't know what it is that makes all of you change-"

It was funny to see how quickly I'd gone from being "one of us," to "one of them."

"- but it has to have something to do with water. Think about it, Boss. How dried out they are; how much everyone sweats before they turn. You just drank four *pounds* of water. It even suggests why they eat us. Our blood; the fluid it holds. They need it. Something about it keeps them going. Do you understand?"

Larry waited with urgent impatience, hands held imploringly at his sides.

"Wow," I said, taking another, more controlled, sip from the jug. "I don't think I've ever heard you say that much at once." Larry deflated like a balloon with a slow leak.

"I believe you, Larry," I said to salvage his ego. "But it doesn't matter." The old man started to protest, but I cut him off.

"You figured out a cure?" I asked bluntly. I didn't have any hopes to get up, and Larry's silence was answer enough. "Then nothing has changed," I continued, taking one more swig from the bottle. "I need to get back up there."

I took a step, and the world seemed to swim in my vision. I staggered to the side, and if it wasn't for the house I was leaning against I would have fallen once more.

"No," Larry said, a hint of authority coloring his voice as he pulled me upright. "You need sleep. I need some time if I'm going to figure this out. We've got the walls covered, and you're going straight to bed."

Oh, Larry, I thought with a hint of regret (another unnatural emotion for me,) *You're being a great guy, and I appreciate it. You're good for my people. But how eager would you be to help me right now if you knew the truth? There are thousands of deaders around Branberry right now, but they haven't killed any one of us at all. Nancy sacrificed herself, sure, but Janessa- Jenna?- was by my hand. Lewis killed himself, and that kind of falls on me, too, I guess. I know you wouldn't hold me responsible for that, but how would you feel if you knew what I did to Nancy's dog?*

I was hard pressed to argue with him, though. Truth be told, I didn't feel good at all, and sleep sounded like the best word I'd ever heard. I looked around the perimeter. The flames were running high, being fed by the last treasures of the people in my group. Not a single deader had gotten over the walls, and at this point no more were approaching. I could afford a few hours to recharge those ol' dry cells, couldn't I?

"Alright," I conceded, and without another word Larry began to walk me to the house we shared. Everyone on the street was involved in their own tasks, and didn't pay any attention to us as he led me up the driveway.

"Just give me some time," he said softly next to my ear, and the proximity of his voice made me flinch. I was surprised to realize that the side of my face had dipped to rest on his shoulder. Maybe I did need to rest as badly as he suggested. "Hold on as long as you can. I can figure this out."

It was a false hope. He may not have known it, but I did. There was nothing to say, so I didn't. Larry got me into bed, and I couldn't tell whether it was more a matter of him laying me down, or me falling off his shoulder as I slumped into bed. I have a vague recollection of him stripping off my top layer of clothing, his hands covered in blue surgical gloves, and his tired eyes going over my body in a methodical fashion, evaluating the extent of my injuries. He spent a few minutes checking the rotten bite mark on my arm, his brow furrowed. I couldn't tell you how long he stayed. I was asleep within moments of my head hitting the pillow.

Have you ever had a dream that forces you to wake up immediately? Maybe of dying or falling? Or maybe not even a dream, but a loud sound in another room. The familiar cry of a child, the abrupt ring of an alarm clock or cell phone. Whatever it could be, but *that sound* that causes you to rocket from the deepest recesses of slumber into alertness? We've all had them, I'm sure, and I was greeted by *that sound* as I slept off the longest day of my life.

While most of *those sounds* are hard to place upon waking- your mind is foggy, your eyes are gummy, you're trying to orient yourself- mine was damn near unmistakable, pulling me from slumber and forcing me to sit up in bed. It was a sound like no other; a sound that couldn't be imitated, duplicated, or mistaken for anything other than exactly what it was. It was the sound of a rifle clacking shut as a bullet slid into the chamber.

I was upright in bed before my eyes were even open. It wasn't that I was unfamiliar with the sound of guns, but, well, when you hear *that sound* that close to you, it catches your attention. Part of my mind automatically assumed that the retort of a shot was bound to follow. As it turns out, I wasn't too far off.

Frankie was standing at the foot of my bed, looking down at me with a rifle in his hands.

My brother in law didn't say anything, but I saw the grim, flat look on his face. I knew why he was here: he'd made up his mind, and had come to do what needed to be done. In the early days, this had been my job, but given the circumstances I could see why he'd taken the responsibility on himself. He didn't move, allowing me to orient myself and wake up fully. I decided to take my time about it.

Dim light was seeping in through my window, telling me that I'd been asleep for several hours. I estimated it to be around 6 a.m. After the rigors of the previous day, I expected my body to be nothing but one massive ache of squalling pain. The reality was quite the opposite. I felt nothing at all. My entire body was numb. Not the tingling numb of a limb that had fallen asleep. No, I felt no sensation whatsoever. Anywhere. I looked down at my arm, noting in a detached way that the sheets of my bed were saturated with sweat.

If it had looked bad last night, my left wrist was worse, now. My shadowed veins were swollen and bulging against my skin. The skin had lost the redness of inflammation, but had taken on a distinctively sallow, unhealthy sheen. Around the location of the bite itself I could see small mounds- like ant bites- that I knew from experience would eventually open up into weeping pustules and sores. I sighed, and looked past Frankie through my open bedroom door. Larry was standing in the hallway, peeking his head around the corner. The pharmacist looked sad and abashed, with deep circles under his eyes. I doubt he'd gotten any sleep last night.

"Sorry, Boss," our bush doctor said in a regretful tone. "I couldn't stop him."

"It's all right, Larry," I said as comfortingly as I could. I don't know how successful I was. "Don't worry about it."

The pharmacist bobbed his head in apology, and then ducked away. I reached over to my nightstand and grabbed the still half-filled jug of water from the previous night, taking a few huge gulps. God, it tasted good. I screwed the cap back on- which was more difficult than I would have thought, since I couldn't feel my fingers- and looked up at the spectre over me.

"Mornin', Francis," I said amiably. My friendly demeanor had no effect on him.

"I gotta put you down, Cleet."

I nodded, wobbling as I stood up. I had no sensation in my legs, so I had to guess when I had them in the right position. This was going to take some getting used to.

"You know I don't want to, right?" he asked. His face may have had the flat eyed look he adopted when he turned his emotions off, but I could see a glimmer at the back of his eyes. I'd known Frankie a long time. We'd been in some rough patches together, and it was moments such as those that really taught you who someone was. He truly didn't want to do this, but it was his duty. I didn't fault him for it.

"I know," I said, standing in front of him. I waited for my head to explode, wondering what it would feel like, but he didn't raise his rifle.

"You're dangerous," he continued, almost like he was trying to convince himself of the necessity of the action. "You killed Nancy. I didn't like her none, but G'dammit, she was one of us. We was supposed to protect her, that was our job! Your job!"

"I know," I said a third time. "It had to be done, though. It was the only way I could get the girl back."

Frankie's lips tightened, but the barrel of the rifle still didn't budge. This wasn't working. Frankie knew what he needed to do- he'd done it before- but he was struggling, now. He needed an incentive.

"I killed Jaime-Lynn, too," I admitted. I was glad I was able to remember her name this time. It would have seemed ingenuine if I'd forgotten, again. "She walked in after I'd helped Nancy find her purpose. I had to take care of it."

Surprise flashed across Frankie's face. So; he hadn't known. Surprise quickly turned to horrified shock, and then to cold anger.

"That girl never did anything wrong besides put her face between the wrong set of thighs."

Now it was my turn to be shocked. I thought that I'd been the only one to know about that little tid-bit. See, I told you Frankie was much smarter than he presented himself to be. But he still hadn't raised that damn gun, yet. I sighed. I was going to have to take care of this myself.

"Let me help," I said as gently as I could. Holding my hands out in front of me, making no sudden movements, I reached down slowly to wrap my fingers around the barrel of his rifle. A brief flutter ran through Frankie- it was ingrained in him not to let a potential hostile touch his weapon- but he didn't resist as I lifted the muzzle. I guided it slowly, not making any aggressive movements, and placed the mouth of the barrel against my forehead.

"I killed Nancy. I killed Jaime-Lynn. Lewis killed himself over it. I gutted Chartreuse and fed him to the deaders." Saying it all out loud, I almost felt like a Confession, like I was seeking absolvement. "I'm infected, and it's burning through me faster than I thought it would. I did what I did for a reason, but I know that I never would have done it if I didn't have the virus rotting my brain from the inside out. My time is almost up, Lewis is gone, and we have a hell of problem on our doorstep. You're in charge now, Francis. Everyone is going to need you. Lacy is going to need you. Now is when you put your dip in your lip, and remind yourself that you're a man; that you do the things that need to be done, whether you want to or not."

"Do what you need to do. It's okay."

Frankie hesitated, but then his eyes went fully flat. He tucked the butt of the rifle into his shoulder, and his finger curled around the trigger. I looked up, saw him staring down at me along the sight, and then closed my eyes. It was time.

"Please don't," a soft voice whispered from the doorway.

Frankie and I both had the same knee jerk reaction, twisting our heads around to look towards the source. I opened my eyes, releasing the barrel of his weapon, and the muzzle drifted away from my head.

Avery stood in my bedroom doorway, garbed in a tattered night shirt that had seen better days. She hadn't made a single sound that either Frankie and I had heard, but there were fresh tear tracks down her solemn cheeks.

"Don't," she whimpered, giving a sniffle. "You can't."

I didn't know whether she was talking to me, or my brother in law.

"Get outta here, Avery," Frankie said harshly, turning to look back down on me across the sight on his barrel. "Get back home to Lacy."

"Go on, kid," I said softly, echoing Frankie's sentiment. "Do what your dad says."

The word just slipped out. I hadn't given it much thought, hadn't meant to say it and put that mantle of both of them, but it was too late. Frankie didn't seem to register it, but the effect on Avery was immediate and shocking.

"He's not my dad!" she shrieked, her face contorting in sudden fury as her voice rose to a decibel level that only teenage girls and 80's rockstars seemed capable of. "My dad is *dead!* And I'm *glad!* He only tried to kill us once, but he hurt us all the time! He hurt us every day, and if I tried to stop him, he hurt me the most! Mommy never did anything! She said it was our fault for making him angry, and then he'd hurt her, too!"

Huh. I hadn't seen that one coming. Frankie and I both stood in stunned silence at the revelation. I hadn't known her parents on more than a friendly wave sort of level, but until things had gone ass up, the five of them had been the picture perfect image of the idyllic family. The tears on Avery's reddened face and her heaving chest told me the truth, though. She'd been protecting her younger siblings when I'd put her parents down, and was the only one that ever made eye contact with adults. With me. The new information changed nothing about the current circumstance, however.

"Avery," I began, speaking a little more forcefully, "get out of-"

"No! No one ever helped us until you!" She screamed, refusing to be interrupted. She turned her puffy eyed, snot nosed face to my assault rifle wielding brother. "And you."

I looked the child in the eye, and as my eyes squinted in understanding,

I saw her, truly saw her, for the first time. Aside from the world she lived in, she was the picture of a typical teenage girl. Temper tantrums, sense of entitlement, overly emotional, tousled hair ... but looking at her eyes- into her eyes- I saw it.

There was darkness, there, and it was a darkness I recognized. It was an unquantifiable thing, but I recognized it, nonetheless.

Avery was like me.

Maybe not yet, though. In this profound, poignant moment, I realized that she hadn't gone over the edge yet. But the edge of the cliff was there, right beneath her toes, and it was a very real possibility. The type of possibility that would turn into a reality if, say, she watched the closest thing she had to a father kill the soon to be deader that she looked at as her own personal hero. But she was no Lois Lane, I was no alien from another planet, and this story didn't have a happy ending.

I couldn't let this happen. Not just for Avery, but for Frankie, too. I knew that I could eventually goad him into doing what he knew needed to be done, but the action would leave a scar on him. It would scar him in the act, and it would scar him to know he'd done it in front of his little preteen foster daughter. Furthermore, he'd have to deal with the fallout of my sister.

As for what it would do to Avery? There was no way of knowing if she would be as good at controlling and hiding it as I had always been. Frankie and I both knew that it had to be done, though. I accepted that.

The solution was surprisingly simple, and suddenly as plain as day. All ends could be met, and we could all win. Frankie's conscience would be clear, Avery might continue to walk on the good side of sanity for a little while longer, and I could go out the way that I'd first wanted: as a samurai.

"Let me go back over the wall," I blurted into the tense silence of the room. Frankie's eyes flicked to mine. Avery stopped her whimpering, and her silence was somehow more dreadful than her shrieks had been.

"We both know I'm done," I said, and once the admission was past my lips I felt like I had been unburdened. "I don't know how much time I have left before I can't control it, anymore. If you keep the fire going long enough, the walls should hold them back. I'll lead them away, and do what I can. Hell," I said, managing to force a chuckle, "I bet I can get at least two dozen taken care of for you."

Frankie blinked, hesitating. He recognized the implications immediately. The barrel of the rifle started to dip, but then he jerked it back up to his shoulder. "How do I even know you're still you?" he hissed. "How do I know you're not gonna come at me the second I turn my back?" "Don't turn your back, then."

At my quip, some of the tension seemed to seep out of him, but it was replaced by a profound sadness that I appreciated.

"The bullet would be faster," he said. "Less painful."

"Yeah," I agreed with a nod. "But it would also just be a waste of a bullet."

Frankie allowed me to go out the backyard rather than walk through my front door to Branberry's gate. Call me selfish for the secrecy, but the only thing I'd ever really taken pride in was my work as an Exterminator. More than that, only two people knew about my current state, and I wanted to keep it that way. I didn't want any of the others to witness my walk of shame. I didn't want Lacy to see me like this. She'd figure it out eventually, but I didn't want it to be right now.

Larry had managed to convince Avery to leave before my exit. The little girl had stared at me with blurry, red rimmed eyes, but hadn't said anything before allowing Larry to shuffle her out. It was probably for the best, and I guess there was nothing that really needed to be said. I realized what she was now- but what I hoped she'd never become- and she knew that I was … fond … of her. That had been enough for both of us.

"Here, Boss," Larry had said after the child departed, gesturing to a jug of water that could have been a twin to the one I was carrying with me. I held up my own quarter-full gallon in response, letting him know that I was set. The jittery pharmacist nodded. "I'll put one up on the wall each day at dawn, just in case, you know, you need it."

I gave him my thanks. While I had noticed that my fever had receded once I'd begun consuming the water, the result of the virus would still run its course. Besides, we both knew that it didn't matter, anyway. The virus wouldn't be what put me down, and I wouldn't be coming back tomorrow morning for the drink.

That had been all the farewell between me and the first immigrant to Branberry before Frankie and I had headed to the backyard. I headed over to the corner of the cinderblock wall, preparing to climb over, the water bottle dangling from my right hand. My walking was still a little clunky, but I'd figured out how to place my steps quickly enough. Frankie followed me like a shadow.

"Give me a boost?" I asked him. Whether I was infectious to the touch yet didn't matter anymore. After Frankie and I had reached our agreement, I'd changed into a new pair of jeans and hooded sweatshirt. I'd placed my expensive, borrowed shoes carefully in my closet, and then strapped on my boots, tucking the hem of my pants in before lacing them up. His skin wouldn't come in contact with mine.

Frankie obliged, lacing his fingers together into a stirrup the same way he always had, and I stepped into his grip. He lifted, and I hoisted myself up until I could set the water bottle on the edge with one hand, and grab the lip of the wall with the other. Bracing my legs against the wall, I shimmied myself up.

"You sure you don't want the Sig back?" Frankie asked as I stood. We'd made a pitstop in the garage before my little adventure, and he handed me up a gooseneck crowbar and long necked carpenter's hammer.

"Nah," I said. "You're gonna need it more than I will, I'd imagine. Tell my sister I love her."

Frankie nodded. There were no "man hugs," this time, and I couldn't blame him. I took a final gulp from the water bottle, and then poured the remaining contents onto the flames. It wasn't enough to put them out, but they did sizzle and drop considerably for a brief moment, giving me enough of a space to not burn myself.

Taking the crowbar and hammer in hand, I jumped over Branberry's wall for the final time.

I couldn't really tell you what I was anticipating to happen when my feet landed on the other side. It had been a whole eighteen minutes since Frankie had woken me in such a jovial manner, most of which period of time I'd been distracted by other things. Not to say my coming excursion hadn't crossed my mind. Quite the contrary; I'd run dozens of different scenarios through my head as I'd changed and gathered my things. None of them ended any way other than I expected, but all were vastly different. Only two of them really seemed to hold any traction:

Scenario 1(a): The deaders swarm me as soon as my feet touch down, and rip me apart moments after I hit the ground.

(This struck me as something very close to what would have happened on television. I don't want to admit it, but given the circumstances, they might have been right.)

Scenario 1(b): My ankles break on impact as I hit the ground. I wouldn't feel it, of course, but would still topple, nonetheless. Then, I'd be forced to crawl around in worthless humiliation until Scenario 1 (a) took place.

-Or-

Scenario 2: I throw myself at the deaders. They turn their milky eyes to me and charge as one howling horde. I roar back, and run to meet them. I dash as fast as I can like a lone Ronin meeting the advance of an enemy clan. I'd proudly raise my claw hammer high, and take down as many as I could before the inevitable came to be.

Of all the possibilities I'd run through my mind, I far preferred Scene 2. Sadly, it didn't come to pass. I kept my footing and the structural integrity of my bones when I landed, but found myself curiously devoid of the playmates I had anticipated.

It was still early in the morning- I checked my watch, which I'd strapped on as I'd gotten dressed, and the monogram said 6: 28- but the sun was high enough above the edge of Sunrise Mountain for me to have a clear view of my surroundings. Despite that I hadn't been eaten alive yet, the circumstances were grim indeed.

It had been hard to tell during the night, but we'd all known that there were hundreds, possibly *thousands,* of deaders surrounding us. My clear view in the early morning told me that we hadn't been too far off the mark. Now, I wouldn't call myself an expert at counting large quantities of things in rapid moments, but looking out beyond the desert perimeter of Branberry- at the staggering number of zombies ambling around or standing transfixed- I figured that fifteen hundred or so fit the bill well enough.

I'm sure that doesn't sound like too many. After all, there were three hundred and eighty thousand Axis troops defending the shores of Normandy, and the Allied forces still succeeded. The Battle of Gettysburg saw fifty-one thousand casualties, and the Union still came out on top. Hell, even General George Custer faced roughly three thousand Sioux tribesmen in the Battle of Little Bighorn.

But we all know how "Custer's Last Stand" turned out.

None of this was the scary part, though. The *scary* part was how they had formed themselves up. Despite the fact that a great many of them were still shambling and stalking back and forth as we'd always known them to do, each and every one was lined up at the edge of the desert perimeter that had been cleared away from Branberry's walls. None of them were going towards the flames, and they were well out of distance.

Most of them still seemed mindless. If they didn't have something to attract their attention, they were little better than automatons, like a child's wind up cymbal monkey. But even those that were still moving around stayed behind an invisible line in the sand that could have been drawn by a pencil.

The most truly terrifying part, though, were those that Frankie and I had established as the "thinkers." These weren't shambling; they weren't rambling. They weren't fighting; they weren't biting. They did not like green eggs and ham; they did not like them, Sam I Am.

The Thinkers had gathered around the dusty Dakota from yesterday, but gathered was too loose of a term. They weren't just in a bunch; no, they'd formed themselves into a rough triangle- rank and file- like a zombie version of Chinese checkers. Of course, I don't ever recall the blue marble prepared to eat the red marble as soon as it had a chance, but I think you get my point.

They stood together, a mixed batch of males and females, not moving at all. It was like looking at a wax museum, if wax figurines could focus their lifeless eyes on precisely the same point. Each and every one was focused on Branberry. Even from this distance, I could hear one give a short, low bark, that was answered by another in their group. A second ticked by, and a third gave a low cough, only to be echoed by the female that was standing at the point of the triangle.

Don't tell me how I knew, but they were *fucking talking to eachother.*

They were communicating in that group, formulating some sort of gameplan, and no matter what it was, it didn't bode well for the little cul de sac that held their focus.

If I was going to accomplish anything worthwhile, it was going to be there. It broke my emotionless heart to admit it, but Branberry was most likely doomed. If I wanted to give them as much of a chance as possible- whether to survive, or to flee- it would best be accomplished by doing as much damage as I could to that "Think Triangle." The problem was, how I could get there? The dusty Dakota was well over a hundred yards away from me. If I tried to get that close to them, I'd be seen, and we all know how that scenario plays out. It was in that short moment of consideration, where I considered my best approach, that Lady Luck winked at me.

An unexpected black shadow moved distantly to my right, at just the proper height to cut off the morning rays of the sun peeking over the mountain tops. I squinted at first, but the shadow cut off the beams of sun glinting into my eyes.

"Screeeech, screeeech, screeeech!"

The loud, ululating shrill cut through the morning like a butcher's knife. As one, the eyes of every deader I could see looked towards the piercing sound. The unity that they showed in their movements was almost uncanny, and I was once again forcibly reminded of a flock of birds. My eyes followed the sound as well, and I saw that the half glimpsed shadow on the wall wasn't a shadow at all.

It was Sister Tracy, standing atop the wall, still bedecked in her black habit and gown. She had her panic whistle tucked tightly in between her shriveled and puckered lips, blowing as hard as her aged lungs could.

Now, I thought, *this is my chance. If I'm gonna take out the Think Triangle, this is my shot.*

I ran towards the Dakota as hard as my numb legs would allow. The gravel crunched beneath my boots, and- gangly and awkward or not- I was shocked by how fast I was moving. I covered the distance between the wall and the Dakota at a pace that an Olympic sprinter would have envied. My hammer and crowbar dangled in my hands, and I wasn't even remotely aware of the vertible rainfall of sweat dripping from me like a squadron of paratroopers.

Given more time, maybe I could have formulated a plan; found a way to be sneakier, more subtle about it. But I'd always approached deaders with the same mindset that an oncologist might approach cancer: you can tickle it with a feather, but smashing it with a hammer is generally more effective.

I dropped my shoulder, and barreled into the blind side of the rank of deaders like a bowling ball spinning into the four pin. The decrepit body I struck flew back, heels leaving the ground, stumbling into a few others in the process. Another single body toppled over, and then I was swinging the hammer and crowbar, in such a haze that I couldn't exactly tell you what was happening.

I cracked skulls with the hammer; crushed ankles with the crowbar. I broke jaws, ripping rotten faces clean off as I screamed out every ounce of fury in me. Deaders were falling like wheat to a scythe, and I dimly realized I might just win my wager with Frankie. I, more than anyone else, knew how dire the circumstances were, but I couldn't deny the savage satisfaction I was taking from this. My face and body were slick with sweat, but it didn't bother me. This was my rush. I was alive, at least for as long as I had left before they recovered from my ambush.

Something was wrong, though, and my confusion set in as the shrill twill of the whistle stopped. I was in the middle of the field of Thinkers, surrounded on all sides, and waiting for the inevitable; waiting for them to converge on me.

But nothing was happening. Not a single deader was paying the slightest bit of attention to me. Beyond the ones that I had taken down and the others that had been forced out of position by the falling bodies of their brothers and sisters, none of the Thinkers had moved. Every single blank, milky eye was turned towards the lone nun standing atop the wall. Not a single one even seemed to notice me.

This pissed me off. I mean, here I am, making my last stand, waiting to die as valiantly as I can, and these things didn't even have the courtesy to pay attention.

Dropping the hammer, I wrapped both hands around the crowbar and started swinging, heaving like a lumberjack chopping wood. Three more deaders fell, spraying me with ichor as they landed with the others on the desert floor. Still, none of them responded to me at all.

I was more than a little angry- this was my moment, after all- and I whirled about in the space of fallen deaders that surrounded me to glare at the old nun. Even at this distance, the details of her face were clear to me. Her features were as cold and hard as they ever were, and as we made eye contact it was clear that she had no love for me; she never had, and had never made too much of a secret of it. Sure, she'd helped me when I'd fallen back over the wall from Rocky Coast, but her concern had always been taking care of her flock. Even a wayward sheep like me.

It was in that moment that sudden epiphany hit me. All of the pieces of the puzzle- a puzzle that I hadn't even realized was being put together- snapped into place, leaving me slack-jawed and stunned. I didn't want to believe it; never thought I would, as a matter of fact, but coincidence can only stretch so far.

God *was* real.

I'd never really given more than a passing thought to the deity. If it was true, the Almighty was nothing more than an absent landlord, or a story to put children to sleep with at night. But in that moment, all the dogma I'd heard my entire life clarified itself into a tangible reality. The constant doctrine of believers rambled through my mind:

God is amongst us. Everything happens for a reason. It's God's will. God has a plan. Put your faith in the Lord, and he'll steer you to where you are supposed to be. Let God be your guidance.

I had always discarded the varied credo of the Bible thumpers as quickly as most people did, but now I was forced to evaluate it in a new light, and it all suddenly made sense. It would be an easy concept to discard, but think about it: of the horde of deaders that surrounded me, not a single one had even deemed to notice my presence. None had even looked at me, as far as I could tell. Even when I'd gone into my suicide frenzy and started hacking them down, not a single one had laid tooth or claw on me.

The reason why seemed fairly obvious in that moment, and I was pretty quick to catch on. The bite on my wrist had infected me, and the virus had run through me quickly; quicker than normal, to be honest. But it was also what was keeping me alive for this moment, though. The deaders didn't see or smell me as prey to be devoured. No; in their rotted brains they saw me as one of their own. You would think that enough of the Thinkers would have recognized me as a threat and banded together to pull me down, but Sister Tracy's whistle was holding their attention.

My mind started churning. I'd always been good at problem solving, so I put a few facts together:

1. The deaders didn't notice me because they thought I was one of their own.

2. The Thinkers had somehow managed to enforce their will on the horde, forcing them to remain behind the cleared perimeter of Branberry's walls.

3. Every single one of the Thinkers around me was focused on the old nun standing atop the wall.

I let my arms fall to my sides, the crowbar hanging in my left hand. I don't know where the hammer had ended up. Deaders were spread around me in a clear space like fallen stalks of grass, but none of the others made a move towards me. It was in that moment that I realized that this was God's plan for me, and it had been designed to perfection. If Branberry was to be saved, there would have to be sacrifices. You can't make an omelet without breaking some eggs, right? The world was a chessboard, and God had chosen me- *me!*- to be his knight.

Man, I thought, awe struck at the revelation. *What an honor. I get to be a hero, a* real *hero, just like Nancy.*

My entire attitude about everything changed in that moment, squealing around like a motorcycle that had made a one hundred and eighty degree turn. I *am* a hero. I *am* a samurai. I *am* a good person.

The sense of urgency- of impending doom- hanging over me evaporated like it had never been there. Like Daniel in the lion's den, *God was with me.*

I strolled in and out between the deaders at my leisure, evaluating them with a speculative eye, and not a single one raised a hand to me. Wrapping my hands about the crowbar, I swung with all my might at the knee of a large male standing in front of me. The cold forged steel connected soundly, crunched, and ripped right through the joint. The now one legged deader flopped to the ground, its milky gaze never leaving the wall where Tracy stood. I felt a smile crack my parched lips. With God on my shoulder, I was obligated to test my luck a little bit, right?

Of course I was. So I did.

I started swinging the crowbar at their hands or ribs, just to see if I would get any response. Nothing. I even spent a few moments giving a half dozen swings to a male, right where the undoubtedly shriveled remains of his testicles should have been. Aside from some broken staggering, he didn't even seem to notice me. Of course he wouldn't, I thought with a chuckle. As far as they could tell, I was invisible, and they couldn't feel pain.

Just like me.

The crowbar had just cranked back to swing again when a random flash of light struck my eyes, drawing me up short. Before this morning's Revelation, I would have called it coincidence, but now I knew better: this was God's will.

God was with me. He believed in me, he'd provided me with a purpose the same way I'd provided Nancy with a purpose, and now he was rewarding me for my dutiful service. The flash came again, glinting in the early morning sun. It was dull, cerulean, and half hidden by a layer of dirt and deader limbs. It was just over *there,* right next to a tire on the Dakota. I shoved a couple of the undead statues around me out of the way and walked towards it.

I reached down to the half buried source of light glinting from beneath the sand. I knew that shape, and I recognized the brilliant face that was looking back up at me. I dropped my gore streaked crowbar to the dirt and forgot about it immediately as I scooped the buried form up in my other hand.

"Ah," I sighed in contentment. "Hey, buddy," I said out loud as I looked into the black eyes of the smiley face sticker of my Happy Bat. I smiled at it, and the decal smiled back. I knew that it was proud of me.

This has been God's plan for you all along, that face seemed to say. *You did what he needed of you, and now, you're the only one that can do what needs to be done to save your people.*

That is the plan, I thought back, humbly. *I just hadn't realized. It's my fault for not believing, but now I know better. Everything happens for a reason.*

We have work to do, the yellow face of my friend said to me, giving me a wink with one black eye.

I know! I agreed, joyous. I took a deep breath, letting it fill my lungs, and when I exhaled I felt the stress and responsibility of the last two days go with it. I was still dying- of that I had no doubt- but I was at peace. Actually, it was better than being at peace.

My Happy Bat was in my hand, and whether I could truly feel the worn leather wrapping in my palm or not, it still brought me a sense of profound familiarity, which in turn brought comfort. I gazed around at the hundreds and hundreds of deaders that surrounded Branberry- none of which could sense me- and heaved a deep sigh of contentment.

'Bout a mile, I thought as the shrill screech of Sister Tracy's whistle resounded once more. I traced my eyes through the uneven field of deaders in front of me, gazing towards the freeway. There were dozens-scores, maybe- in my direct path, but that wasn't going to be an issue. Not for me, at least.

Staggering thirst made the lining of my throat feel like it was lined with burrs, but somewhere up there- beyond yonder, as they say- was a 1987 Daihatsu Surprise with a mostly full bottle of Kentucky's finest in the trunk, brewed from the recipe of Mr. Beam, himself. And to be honest, Late Night Buyer? If today isn't a day for celebration, to indulge in a little bit of redneck good times, I don't know what is. I checked the watch on my wrist, and the monogram read 6:36 a.m.

Shit, I thought, feeling a smile tugging at the corners of my lips. *That's plenty of time.*

I sighed in contentment, whirling the familiar haft of my Happy Bat in my hand as I walked forward. I couldn't hold back the joy in my heart, and my lips puckered as I began to whistle a jaunty tune. It wasn't as good as Guns' N' Roses, but it was pretty close. I took a good grip on my bat, and lined it up at the unsuspecting deader closest to me.

Today was going to be a good day.

Here's a little song I wrote,
You might want to sing it, note for note,
Don't worry;
(Ba-dum-bump, ba-dum-bump, ba-dum-bump)
Be happy.
-Bobby McFerrin

Author Bio

N.D. Mellen hales from Las Vegas with his three children, and is a life long practitioner of combat sport. When his hands weren't in a pair of sixteen ounce gloves, his nose was in a book. The fight scenes were always his favorite.